"Payton, I don't bel[...] be honorable where you are concerned. Do you understand?"

"No, sir." She turned to face him fully and tried to smile, but instead her lip trembled and she shook as one lost in the cold without cape or gloves.

"There is no way for me to keep him from you, save one. If you are in agreement." He took her hands in his. So small and helpless. His stomach churned to think of that man's paws on her.

"You look so stern, Mr. Lambrick. Did I do something to anger you?"

"No. You did nothing wrong. Sit back down. Please." He sucked in a breath and groaned.

"Are you all right? Mr. Lambrick?"

"Payton, I have to say this, no matter how incredulous it may sound. Mrs. Brewster and I have no other solution to offer. Your uncle said he would be back in a fortnight or so. We could try to hide you, but, Payton, if you will marry me, he cannot take you away. Do you understand?"

"Marry you?"

**Books by Linda S. Glaz**

Love Inspired Heartsong Presents

*With Eyes of Love*
*Always, Abby*
*The Substitute Bride*
*The Preacher's New Family*

## LINDA S. GLAZ

is married with three children and three grandchildren and is a complete triple-A personality. How else would she find time to write as well as be an agent for Hartline Literary Agency? If she isn't writing or putting together a contract, you'll find her taking a relaxing bath with her eReader in hand. Life doesn't get much better than that.

# LINDA S. GLAZ

*Bride by Necessity*

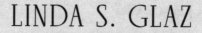

HEARTSONG
PRESENTS

Recycling programs
for this product may
not exist in your area.

™ LOVE INSPIRED BOOKS

ISBN-13: 978-0-373-48712-7

BRIDE BY NECESSITY

www.Harlequin.com

**Printed in U.S.A.**

Defend the cause of the weak and fatherless;
maintain the rights of the poor and oppressed.
Rescue the weak and needy; deliver them
from the hand of the wicked.
—*Psalms* 82:3–4

To my fabulous family who keeps me on track.

# Chapter 1

*Kent Park, England, 1855*

Mist flowed over the sandy hills of Kent Park and settled on the trees like a thick shroud. Payton Whittard tucked her legs closer and shivered. Then, in no time at all, the sun swallowed the mist along with Payton's worries. She jumped to her feet and listened for the sound of wagon wheels. Father and Mother would be here soon, and the noon meal awaited. But she couldn't pull herself from the faint rainbow now forming, offering comfort and hope. She shaded her eyes to soak in the remaining bits of pink and lavender as the last dots of color cleared the sky.

She heard no wagon wheels, no sounds other than the birds crying out and the water rippling. With one last peek over the hills, her gaze locked on the sun as it re-emerged from the bank of clouds, blinding her momentarily.

Suddenly she heard hooves and a shout. "Out of the way!"

Thundering noise encircled her, threatened her in a great cloak of fear. She gasped and searched for cover, stumbling into the gnarled arms of a towering horse chestnut tree. Massive hooves pawed the air inches from her face while deafening grunts poured from the open mouth of a beast. She covered her face with her hands. A hoof grazed her arm and she cried out.

The rider leaped from his mount and landed by her side.

"Where are you hurt?" His hands traced her arms checking for injuries and leaving trails of warmth along her skin. He probed her torn sleeve. "Are you hurt, girl?" When he found nothing amiss, he abruptly turned away, and she backed again into the safety of the tree. "Take care in the future." He reached for the reins as Payton trembled, words far from her mouth. But feelings ever present. Strange, new feelings.

In spite of the control he exhibited over the animal, she withered inside from the beast's wild eyes and stomping hooves. "I am not hurt, sir. Just shaken, Mr. Lambrick." She stretched her hand over her head for her bonnet, but her hair had already tumbled into her face. Tugging fingers through tangled curls, she pushed the waves of hair from her eyes.

"Have you a name?" His dark gaze raked her from her bare feet to her grass-stained skirt and shamed her for being caught in such an unruly manner. "Of course, you're Daniel Whittard's girl. My second cousin by marriage."

Still shivering from fright, she bit her lip and nodded. An attempt to curtsey failed when her legs stiffened beneath her. Her face flamed hot as embers and she blinked. "Yessir. Payton Whittard. Forgive me unsettling your horse."

His hand waved her away. "As long as you are all right." She read curiosity in his eyes.

In spite of her mother's cautions to the contrary, Payton stared. The long, jagged scar that ran across his cheek and through his lip she'd only ever seen from a distance. But it didn't distract from his dark good looks. Silently, he mounted his horse and adjusted the bit. She wondered at the source of his injury, but good manners prevented her inquiring.

He reached up, stippled the scar with tense fingertips, then glanced once more in her direction before nudging the monster's sides. His eyes changed…flickering sparks before his cape swirled around both of them like great black wings. She fancied herself witness to some exotic flying creature, half horse, half frighteningly mysterious man. Her heart skipped a beat from the way he sat his mount as if the two became one the second he fell into the saddle. *Fanciful thinking,* her mother's voice echoed in her head.

Though the young master Lambrick had been nearing twenty when old Master Kent passed away in his sleep, she'd been just a child at the time. She remembered his gloomy features when first he was introduced to her father. Angry perhaps, but angry at what? He had just inherited a great fortune. The rich were a funny lot. For the past ten years she had paid particular attention to staying out of his way.

With the fright behind her, she condemned her laziness and tucked her skirt once again into the waistband. Hopefully no one else would come along. Mother continually warned her to behave like a lady whenever she was out, but stumbling over the heaviness of a straggling, wet skirt didn't make sense.

A glance toward the cottage brought her up short—no time for more daydreams. Her parents would be arriving any minute after a day in Colchester, and hot tea must be prepared. While she hurried to the house, she continued to gaze over her shoulder in Lambrick's direction. Out of breath, she skirted the stone path and sprinted straight for the door. One last glimpse showed him at the crest of the hill overlooking his vast property. A dark silhouette, frightening and out of reach. Out of reach, but not out of mind.

Busy with her duties, Payton watched the afternoon sun come and go. Dusk settled across the valley without a sign of her parents. Father or no father, chores must be finished. As the dimming light scaled the peaks, she fed the puppies and nestled them onto freshly heaped straw next to their mother, Chloe. How her mother disliked that she helped her father raise the hounds.

She milked Lila, the Guernsey, and replated the meat, fresh bread and apples she had planned for their noon meal. She shivered at her parents' unusual absence. Any minute now, father's capable hands should appear on the reins while Mother jostled her baby brother, Timothy, on the same ample lap that had comforted her as a child.

Fire snapped in the grate and she rubbed her hands together, forcing warmth into her fingers. It was strangely cold even for this late in October. Or was she merely feeling a chill because of her parents' tardiness? She leaned her head on her palms and peeked through the window at the far side of the table. She opened a book, but before she set to reading, a solitary figure passed by and she heard the crackle of leaves under heavy feet. A rap at the door. When she gazed through the window again, she spied the outline of a big man.

Without her parents at home, she hesitated. Finally, she eased the door just a crack and then opened it when she recognized Mr. Kenny, head groomsman for Kent Park. He clapped weathered hands together and slapped his arms against the night chill until she opened the door wider and motioned him in. "Mr. Kenny? What are you doing here?"

Hat in hand and with head bowed, he stood for a moment, shifting from foot to foot, saying nothing. Then he reached for her hands. His frown quickly gave way to compassion. A shaky voice pressed through his lips and punctuated each word. "I'm sorry, child. That I am. You'd better sit ya down."

She gazed into his weathered face. Her heart hammered at her own fear clearly reflected in his eyes.

"I have bad news for ya."

Jonathan tugged his greatcoat closer and gazed at the small hands, no strangers to hard work, as the girl dropped a wild pink rose atop each grave. Miss Whittard's father, her mother and her brother. All gone. If he hadn't traveled out again after dinner, he might not have discovered them.

He shook his head. All three had been killed when their cart rolled off the road into the gully some twenty feet deep. Only the baby had survived a few minutes. Not long enough for Jonathan to fetch help. The accident had happened in the same place where his wife, Alithea, had met the same fate.

He would arrange for Kenny and a dozen or more workers to fill in the crevasse immediately, as he should have before. No one else would die on his land. He wiped a hand across his eyes as if he could stop the scene unfolding in his mind.

The girl's fingers grasped his arm when he offered it, and she gazed at him through tear-filled eyes, pleading for answers. Jonathan had none that would appease Miss Whittard. Only stark reality in the form of wide-eyed pain met his gaze.

"Mr. Lambrick, I appreciate all you did to try and save Timothy. I owe you more than you know, sir. How could they have missed their turn in the daylight? Father has driven that road hundreds of times."

Scrambling for a suitable response as her tears pooled once again, Jonathan straightened. He had only himself to blame. Her pride evident as she looked away, searching her sleeve for a handkerchief, she lowered her gaze. It became obvious she was a very private person as she endured her pain in silence.

Daniel Whittard had saved his father when they were boys and now he would repay the debt. Whittard's wife had been a gentleman's daughter, and he would care for her daughter; he owed them this much.

"It was my fault. That road has been a danger for many years. I am sorry for your loss, Miss Whittard. Where will you go? Have you relatives with whom you might live?"

"No, sir. I had hoped to continue on at the cottage raising father's hounds." Her eyes begged the obvious response. "If you will allow it, of course."

"The land is yours, but a girl living alone is most improper. You must have someone."

"No, sir. You are my only kin…of that I am certain." Her lip trembled and he closed his eyes to collect his thoughts.

When he opened them, she had pulled herself up as

straight as possible, doing her best to hide her fear. Her expression pained him. He would have laughed aloud under other circumstances at one so small trying to stand tall and in control. "Then you'll join us at Kent Hall. Mrs. Brewster will see to your needs."

"And the pups?"

He didn't want a girl underfoot, let alone a house full of yapping puppies. "Not now."

"But, sir. I am afraid I have no choice but to talk about them now. They depend on me. My father depended on me to care for them."

He recognized her anxiety, and in his heart, remembering his own grief, he understood she had faced enough sorrow in the past two days to last a very long lifetime. How could decency allow him to say no? "Very well. We'll fetch the hounds. I'll have Birdie organize a suitable place in the stable. I'll send Mrs. Brewster and Mr. Kenny along to assist you after you are settled."

Her appearance, much improved with her skirt over her ankles like a respectable young lady, caught his attention for a moment. What was it about her face that didn't seem at all like a child? How old was she now? Thirteen? Fourteen? Fifteen? He couldn't remember. He only recalled seeing her up close a few years ago when he spoke with her father about training a new hound. Her steps fell heavy for one so small. But she would get used to disappointment just as he had.

"Come along and we'll find you a room." He disengaged her hand from his arm and struggled to interpret her reaction.

"Allow me to stay over the stable. I beg you, sir. I'll not feel at home in the great hall."

He urged her forward. "Be quick about it. I leave for

London today and I am already late starting. I'll not have my charge, my kin, living in the stable like a servant."

She braced her legs, and it struck him she resembled a bantam rooster ready for a fight. "Sir, I cannot live in your home."

"Don't be foolish, child." He couldn't pull the words back, but he wished he had chosen more wisely. Her face fell, tragedy her only companion. "Forgive me. It is late. Emily Brewster will help you." He motioned Emily forward. "Emily, see to Miss Whittard. And *not* in the servants' quarters."

Emily took Payton's arm. "Yessir. I'll settle her in the guest chamber. Miss Anne's rooms, unless you expect her soon."

He swallowed hard and his face tightened. "I do not." He had planned to visit Anne in London, but now the uncertainty drew him up. She hadn't been home to receive him the last two times he had called. In truth, he had been glad. Now this girl. How would he make excuses for one so young residing in his home? But he owed it to the memory of his father and hers. They had been friends in spite of their different stations in life.

The girl would be Emily's to handle. He paid her handsomely to deal with his problems.

After he strode toward the doors of Kent Hall and slipped inside, lightning streaked across the sky and touched down, lighting a patch of wildflowers not far from the house. Jonathan's hands skimmed the window where rain pelted the glass in sheets and threatened the very foundations of the building. With so much rain two days after the last downpour, the road would be steeped in mud. He gritted his teeth; the trip must be put off. He would be stuck in the house playing guardian to young Payton Whittard. With a shake of thunder, the window quivered under his fingers. His lip curled back and a groan racked his body. The last thing he wanted was a female, young or old, interrupting the routine of his home. Not even Anne, if truth be known. Though if she had her way, she would be the mistress of Kent.

Wooden doors at the entrance of the dark, foreboding structure towered over Payton's head. Her stomach churned. Ivy trailed over the sill and along the sides in dappled green strands that clung to the chipped edges of stone. She considered stopping to appreciate the delicate tendrils but, instead, she hurried through. As the heavy doors banged behind her, an echo filled the hall. She huddled small aside the indomitable Mrs. Brewster, unsure what to make of this mansion. She hadn't ever seen the likes.

The entrance alone could have comfortably fit her home within its walls at least twice. Silver bowls of flowers adorned decorative wooden tables in the front. She recognized wild roses from the north peak at the end of the creek. Stern-looking stone benches lined the inner side walls, but their velvet cushions provided an inviting air in spite of the shadows flitting through every corner.

What was she doing here? Why couldn't she continue to live at her parents' cottage? Yet there was no arguing with the master of Kent Park. Her father had told her as much at least a dozen times. He had also told her Jonathan Lambrick had a far-reaching reputation as an honest and fair man. She held back tears that burned her eyes. She would do as Mrs. Brewster directed until she gained the courage to face Lambrick and return to her home.

In an attempt at tidying herself, Mrs. Brewster brushed raindrops from her creased forehead and pushed back tight, gray curls. She hurried Payton through the entranceway where a manservant waited to take their cloaks.

"Thank you, Duncan." Mrs. Brewster nodded her gratitude.

A Persian runner snaked to a winding staircase of deepest mahogany. Lambrick must have a team of servants, for the wood of each step shone with brilliance. One of the hounds, a runt she had helped her father whelp, stretched atop the landing and wagged his tail once she arrived at his side. "Hunter. My, you've grown up handsome and you are at home here, aren't you, boy?" He pressed into her hand, lapping at her fingers. "You remember me, do you?"

She ruffled the brown velvety ears and rubbed the hairs around his muzzle. Contentment filled her as she recalled the day she had helped her father deliver the litter. Hunter, so small and helpless, had fit neatly into her palm, seemingly far too small to survive. The dog had; her father hadn't. She closed her eyes and crumpled to the floor. The dog licked the salty tears from her face as she stroked his fur. Here was the runt with huge paws that bespoke his maturity and strength.

Hunter nuzzled her shoulder. "Such a lovely welcome." She choked back further tears and glanced away. Clutching her cape around her, she became lost in the warmth. Like her mother's arms. Arms that would never embrace her again. A face she would not see again and lips that had brushed her cheek good-night for the last time. Payton gathered Hunter into her arms and sobbed against his coat. He stood patiently as she used him to struggle to her feet. "There's a fine fellow."

He followed at her side as she traipsed after Mrs. Brewster, who pretended not to notice the display. Past the landing and along the tapestry-laden hallway into the east wing they marched. Even through tear-filled eyes, she recognized this could not be the servants' section.

"This portion of the floor will be for you alone, dearie. No one to bother you unless we have guests." Mrs. Brewster gestured along the hallway, and her voice resounded against the fine wooden panels.

The housekeeper then admitted her to an elaborate guest suite, *definitely* not servants' quarters. The bedroom offered soft yellow papered walls. A spread of cream-colored tatting covered the four-poster bed like a spider's web of silk. Tiny knots intertwined to form the delicate pattern dainty to the touch. Payton sat, losing herself in a softness she had never known. Was this what it meant to be rich? Mother had tried to explain to her what money could do, but she had not known firsthand the kind of life from which her mother had come. She always thought her family rich because of their love. Love of each other, love of God and love of life.

A small sitting room in browns, deep red and cream adjoined the bedroom through a closet large enough to hold the clothes of every member of her family. Centered in the room was a darling settee in damask far too beautiful for sitting.

Not wanting to dillydally, she retraced her steps to the bedroom where Mrs. Brewster, still huffing from the climb up the long staircase, had cracked opened Payton's satchel. She pulled personal items from it with slow hands, and Payton blushed at her boldness. She wasn't used to other people handling her things. Had life been lavish like this for her mother before she met and married her father? He'd been given a small property by old Mr. Lambrick when he was young, and then he'd married the distant cousin of the Lambricks, Mary Kent, her mother.

The quiet, personal life in the cozy cottage was more to Payton's liking than this cold mansion.

"I'll take care of my own undergarments, Mrs. Brewster."

The old face lifted with a scowl that could not be misunderstood. "Very well. You should change into your best dress for dinner. Mr. Lambrick will be home tonight after all, and he always dresses for dinner."

Payton swallowed over a lump. Dinner with Mr. Lambrick. She had expected her life to be with the servants. Her thoughts drifted to the only good dress she owned, the one on her back. Jutting her chin to quell the tears, she said, "This *is* my best dress, Mrs. Brewster. I've never found much need for silk gowns when I'm milking the cow and slopping hogs."

With cheeks plump and red as an apple, Mrs. Brewster's eyes softened into genuine kindness. "I meant no harm. Perhaps you'd like to freshen up then. I'll fetch you a pitcher of water."

The woman was only trying to help, and Payton bit her lip. Her mother would be shamed by Payton's rude behavior. She tried to smile, but nothing came of it other than an uncomfortable grimace. She reached for the wrinkled hands knotted with old age. "I should ask your forgiveness. Shall I put my things away, or will I be staying here just for the night?"

"Foolish girl. This is your home now. Do whatever you wish. Use whatever you like." Mrs. Brewster ambled through the doorway. "I may be able to locate a few suitable gowns for your use but not this night."

"May I clear this case for my books? I study each day and I would prefer them near me."

"Whatever pleases you," she said as she left the room.

After a minute, Mrs. Brewster returned to the room,

her hands straddling her hips and her mouth a line of frustration. "I think you should understand, miss. Mr. Lambrick is a generous man. Never knew him to turn anyone out. He respected your father. He'll raise you up just fine. Don't you worry."

Payton lifted her chin again and tightened her lips. "Raise me? You talk as if I'm nothing but a child."

# Chapter 2

The storm lessened outside, but the storm in his heart still roared in his ears. A ward. Jonathan did not want to take care of a girl. She would be a reminder. A horrid reminder of the life he had lost. By now, he might have had a daughter of his own, or perhaps even a son to carry on the Lambrick name.

He groaned. That would not happen now. He had only memories.

The smells before him did not entice him to eat. His stomach churned at the thought of a heavy meal. A succulent ham surrounded by spicy, sweet apples had been placed there by Emily Brewster in an attempt to tantalize him, but the events of the past twenty-four hours bothered him more than he liked to admit. Where was the girl? Perhaps she had decided to eat with the servants. If so, he would have to put a stop to such foolishness. He intended to see she was brought up a proper lady, not like an urchin running about as he had seen her do on so many occasions.

He lifted his glass and allowed a small sip to pass his lips. He set it back on the table when Emily entered. "Where is Miss Whittard?" he asked.

"Don't be cross with the child. She has been through a great deal and will no doubt take time settling in. I have carried her a pitcher of water to wash her face."

"Emily, you and I both know there's no sense in her feeling sorry for herself. Pity is a tough master. She'll have to accept her new circumstances and move forward with the living. Isn't that what you taught me?" He heard Payton's steps too late.

A gasp followed by undeniable courage in her face moved him. "I will accept whatever is necessary, Mr. Lambrick. I realize the choice is not my own. Yet know this—I have never been one to waste time on self-pity. Thank you for offering your home, but I intend to return to the cottage in the morning. This arrangement simply will not do. I shall have to learn to take care of myself."

She spoke well. He indicated a chair. "Sit down. We'll discuss your circumstances after dinner. You haven't eaten today, have you?" He turned to Emily, who immediately heaped slices of ham, potatoes and apples onto a plate and placed it in front of Payton along with the glass of fresh milk. The girl seemed well-fed, but he understood the importance of nourishment in times of difficulty.

Payton frowned at him. "You're not eating?"

"I finished long ago," he lied. No need to explain himself to a child. She thought she had lost loved ones? *He* had lost loved ones. And the weight of guilt fell heavily on his shoulders.

* * *

On closer inspection, Payton recognized a different hunger on Jonathan's face. But for what, she wasn't sure. She shook her head. What did it matter? As the master of Kent Park and this great hall, he owed her no explanations. Nor was it her business to address him on such a serious matter. No sense worrying and guessing about someone with whom she did not plan to spend another day, but the words escaped her before she could stop them. "Forgive my saying so, sir. Your plate is quite empty. And I must say, clean as anything."

His face darkened and his eyes narrowed. She swallowed hard as he pressed his hands against the table. "My eating habits, young lady, are none of your concern." Lambrick stood and strolled to the window, ending any further discussion of his dinner.

Payton, sorry she'd spoken out of turn, lowered her gaze. He had offered his home and his table, and she was allowing her grief to speak before she thought. She closed her eyes and calmed her emotions. "Please accept my apology. And I appreciate Mrs. Brewster for cooking the meal." Her mother had often warned her of speaking instead of listening. Payton swallowed against the words she longed to say, that she didn't want to be here any more than Lambrick wanted her here.

"I am sorry if I speak out of turn, but you look hungry. I know I've disrupted your comfortable ways by being here, and I'm terribly sorry."

"Give it no thought." His hand waved away her words as if she were nothing more than a stable boy.

Face burning with indignation, she crossed her arms. A noise from outside drew her attention. She tilted her head toward the door. What was that odor? "Do you smell smoke?"

* * *

Jonathan spun about, cocking his head to the side. "Emily?" He stepped nearer to her.

The woman planted her hands on her hips, her favorite posture, and gestured with her eyes in the direction of the back room. "I never can trust that girl in the kitchen. Clarisse will burn the hall down around us." Her steps clattered on the floor as she marched back to the kitchen.

Jonathan gasped. No, it couldn't be. He crossed the floor to the window once again. Searching through the darkness, he choked. Flames flickered in the distance. The Whittard cottage. He turned to the girl, trying his best to remain calm. "If you will excuse me, I must tend to a matter. Please, Miss Whittard, remain seated. Finish eating. Mrs. Brewster will see to your needs when she returns."

Once clear of the house, he dashed to the stable. The girl would have nothing but the small satchel she had brought from her home if he didn't hurry. This bad luck was turning into a nightmare. A nightmare he wanted no part in fixing. But here he was.

Arriving at the cottage at the same time as half a dozen of his tenants, he directed them in putting out the blaze, but already fire had consumed most of the interior of the structure, the outside charred and circled with skeletal bushes and leaves of ash. He kicked aside an old humpback trunk carried out by one of the men. The top fell into pieces and the glassware inside was nothing but a bundle of shards.

"The dogs! We haven't moved them yet!"

Jonathan whirled around to see Payton clawing at the lady next to him. "We have to save the animals!"

Jonathan yelled at his tenant, old Mrs. Grandy. "Hold her back. Don't let her near the fire." He moved quickly in their direction.

As he tried to reach her, Payton vaulted from Mrs.

Grandy's grasp straight to the shed where the hounds were kept. "Kenny, get her. Take her now!" Lambrick knew the animals were already gone. From the look of it, the shed may have been where the fire started. Boys playing with a lantern, lightning from the storm—he couldn't be sure which.

"My dogs! Oh, dear Lord, please don't let them die. Help me find them!"

Payton fought against Mr. Kenny, scurrying for the ruins. Before Lambrick could restrain her, she pushed her hands against the charred frame of the doorway and pressed into the smoke-stained wood.

"Payton!"

She tugged at the boards until he reached her side. She faltered at the opening and collapsed in the heat. Scrambling to free her from falling timber, he shoved two men out of the way and dropped to his knees. He cradled her against his shoulder while shouting at Kenny. "Fetch Dr. Finley. She's burned."

"I'll be…fine. Find my…animals."

With gentle fingers, he pushed back the scorched hair around her face and stared into red eyes, wide with fear. Her hands pushed against him as she struggled to get out of his grasp.

"Oh, please free my dogs." Her swollen lids closed against the smoke and heat, tears dribbling from the corners as at last she gave in and stopped fighting him.

Recognizing time was of the essence, Jonathan lifted her easily and ran the entire way to Kent Hall. There was no way any pups had survived that fire.

Strong arms enclosed her, but the pain only increased from the pressure. Heavy footfalls thudded as they neared the hall. Payton's gut wrenched at the smell of her burned skin and hair. Or…the puppies. Without a doubt, they were gone. Her dry, scratchy throat stung when she swallowed. All she had left in the world lay in ruins.

The heat had penetrated her boots as if her skin had melted into the leather. So much pain. She reached up. Brittle ends of scorched hair met her fingers, and she cried over the loss of her one beauty. "What happened to them?"

"Shh. Don't fret now. We need to get you inside."

Words stuck in her throat, and she couldn't bring herself to look up. "Did any of the hounds… Did you—"

"You'll be fine," Mr. Lambrick's deep voice soothed. "Quiet now."

"Please," she buried her face deeper into his chest, "tell me you found them." Her parents gone, her brother, her home. *Please don't let the animals be gone, too.* How could she live without her family? Her precious hounds? She had let her father down.

Spoken with surprising gentleness, his words calmed her. "The men are searching as we speak."

That wasn't the answer she longed for. She pulled her head from his shoulder. "Why has no one lit…any candles?"

Jonathan stared. Candles blazed in the hallway, brighter than the fire they'd just left. Guilt overwhelmed him as he looked into the blank eyes rimmed with patches of raw, red skin. A few more seconds and she would have died in that fire. He must slip her safely into bed. Carrying her up the staircase two steps at a time, he stopped only long enough to shout to Emily Brewster. "The doctor will be here shortly. Send him right up. Fetch water and bandages immediately! The child's hurt. And for heaven's sake, send Birdie to help hunt for those dogs."

He hadn't been a praying man since the death of his lovely Alithea, but with Payton securely in the protection of his arms, he prayed with the heart of a man starving for answers. *Let them find her puppies. Let her have at least that much to sustain her.*

With care, he placed her atop the bed and began peeling away boots that steamed beneath his fingers. Mrs. Brewster entered and thrust him away. "Here now. You'll be waiting below for the doctor. I'll take care of Miss Whittard. Bring the doctor up soon as he arrives."

How much help would the doctor be? "Emily, she said she can't see."

"Go, dearie." Her outstretched finger pointed him toward the door.

Once again taking the stairs two at a time, Jonathan hurried to the entrance. He heard footsteps and expected to find old doc Finley on the stone walk. But instead, Kenny appeared with a sooty face and a scraggly puppy in his arms. Smoke-streaked, it whimpered in his arms. "Just one, sir. Only one and she won't make it through the night, I'm afraid."

Tired of bad pronouncements, Jonathan straightened to his full stature as if that might force away the pup's poor prognosis. "She will if you attend to her. All night, Kenny, if that's what it takes. Payton Whittard must have something by which to remember her family. Tell Birdie to help. He's as good with animals as you. This puppy must live."

He glared out the doors and saw Dr. Finley's carriage arrive as Kenny removed the dog to the stables. Finley followed Kenny's retreating steps with his eyes and hurried from the buggy. "What's this?" He lifted his small black bag. "You brought me all this way to care for a puppy?"

Jonathan's patience wore thin. "No. A girl. Young girl who lost her family yesterday. We buried her people this morning."

"The Whittards?"

"Yes. Their house burned and the girl attempted, unsuccessfully, to save the animals. No more talking. She's upstairs and gravely injured." They didn't need to stand here carrying on a conversation when she fought for her life. He could not be responsible for another girl losing her life on his watch.

"Lead the way."

Jonathan waited in the hallway while the doctor went in. As the doctor attended Payton, Jonathan felt he could stand her cries no more. He needed to be of help. Be sure she was getting the best care possible. He peered through the crack in the door.

Bent over the girl, Dr. Finley slathered Payton's eyes in oil and poured more tepid water over the sheet. "She'll need care all through the night. Mrs. Kirsten is about to bring forth her sixth child and the babe is turned. I'll have to stay with her until she delivers. Just do as I've told you, Mrs. Brewster."

Jonathan stepped through the door. "I'm here. What can I do?"

He glanced in Emily's direction, steering clear of the pain etched on Payton's face. "Emily, fetch one of Anne's nightgowns for her." At least she would be more comfortable in a soft gown.

"No." The doctor shook his head, his big earlobes bobbing like turkey waddles. "Nothing but a dampened sheet under her and one over her. Only wet sheets to keep the burns moist. You understand? Mrs. Brewster, you will need to put this salve on the burns every two hours and moisten the sheets again. Can you and Mr. Lambrick handle it?"

Mrs. Brewster's eyes narrowed as she joined hands to hips again. "I'll be taking care of her, doctor. Mr. Lambrick needn't be in the room at all. Not at all."

Lambrick scowled. He wasn't used to being ordered about. "What's come over you, Emily?" He spoke and his tenants obeyed—period. Why was she behaving so strangely? His hands could smear salve as well as hers.

"No, sir. She's my responsibility and I'll see to her. Give Clarisse orders to handle affairs below while I'm up here. I won't leave Miss Payton's side until she's able to care for herself. And get one of the manservants to see if any of her belongings survived the blaze."

Confusion played in his mind and he ran fingers through his hair. Why was Emily being so secretive about the girl?

Mr. Kenny, seated on a wooden stool near the door of the barn, fumbled with the puppy, lively in spite of her condition. He patted her gently, but she whimpered and scratched at his knobby hands in an effort to escape. The fire hadn't squelched her feisty behavior. She'd been raised by Payton all right.

Kenny held her up for scrutiny. "I do believe she's goin' ta make it, sir. I put a little mud along her side here. Rinsed her eyes so's maybe they'll heal. She's not happy with all the attention, but I think there's a chance she'll survive. And the girl? Miss Whittard?"

Lambrick stared first at the pup and then at Kenny. How should he know? Emily had banned him from the room. So much for her being his ward, but he could not let on he wasn't allowed into a room in his own house. "Same as the puppy. Maybe and maybe not. Time will tell. Mrs. Brewster is with her and said she'll stay by her side until we know more." He knelt by the stool and touched the velvety nose now crusted with mud. Well, Kenny allowed him to help, at least.

"Emily's a fine lady." Kenny nodded, holding on with all his might to keep the pup quiet as she clawed at him to be let down. "If anyone can see the girl through this, Emily Brewster can."

With little effort, Jonathan drew the anxious pup into his arms and stroked the soft fur left along the back of the pup's neck and shoulders. "Poor little mite. You're lucky your mistress cared enough to dig around for you." Black eyes stared at him, and her tongue lapped at his hands. "Where did you discover her, Kenny?"

"Scramblin' out of that half-charred wood. The miss saved her life all right. If she hadn't loosened the boards, the pup wouldn'ta found her way out."

Jonathan thought about what she had sacrificed to save this dog, pictured her small hands clamoring at the scorched boards to find her precious puppies. Such determination for one so young. He swallowed hard. He had been as determined at life once upon a time. When had he lost that strength of character? He'd lost his desire to live when Alithea died. When she… He handed the puppy back to Kenny and rose.

"Stay with her. All night if you must. This animal cannot die."

Like monsters tormenting her in the bowels of the earth, hands plucked at her, causing more pain. "Please, leave me. Stop touching me."

Fingers wiped her forehead and offered relief at last with cool water. "There, now."

"That hurts. What…happened?" Was someone really there or had she imagined the cool hands and soft voice?

"I will stay by you. You have nothing to fear, dearie. The master's gone to the stable and there's no one to find out."

That familiar voice again. Mother? "Find out…what?"

"I'll keep your secret."

Foolish talk. Payton squinted through eyes stinging from salty tears. Everything blurred before her. Not her mother—Mrs. Brewster from Kent Hall. "My secret?"

"Dearie, you're no child."

It was so dark and now this woman's foolish talk. "I think I…remember telling all of you…that."

A soft hand patted her arm, then spooned liquid into her mouth. "You did indeed. I suppose we weren't listening."

"No one here…ever listens." The taste stuck to her tongue and she shivered. Secrets. She kept no secrets.

"Try and sleep." Pieces of hair stuck in her eyes, causing them to burn when Mrs. Brewster smoothed her brow. "The laudanum will help to ease the pain. Are you comfortable?"

"Not very. I'm sorry to complain."

"Child, you have been through a great deal. You may say whatever you like to old Emily, here."

"Emily?" A shiver racked her and her teeth chattered when she spoke. "I'm cold. Could I…have a quilt?"

"Doctor says nothing but the damp sheets. For the burns. We can't let the material stick to your skin. But I'll fetch another and put it on top of this one. You try and sleep. And rest those eyes. In no time at all, you'll be right as rain."

"Yes, ma'am. But the hounds. Did they…find any of

the hounds?" She stifled a yawn, fighting to stay awake until she heard about her animals.

"That will have to wait 'til morning. You are all that's important right now."

Payton did her best to lie still under the sheets but felt her skin pull against it, and she cried with the sharp pain. Even when she stayed as still as a fat tick, the ache was more than she could bear.

One day at a time.

Her father had taught her early on when she first lost a favorite animal that difficulties came easier if you dealt with them one day at a time. It must be the same with pain. Well then, she would endure this torture one miserable day at a time.

Daubed in mud from the puppy, Jonathan landed on the top step seconds before Mrs. Brewster eased into the hall and closed Payton's door in his face. His face heated. "Why aren't you in there caring for her?" His hands brushed at his jacket, disliking disorder of his person even in times of stress.

"Shh. Mr. Lambrick, she's sleeping. Doesn't need us hovering. If I might be presumptuous, you don't look well yourself." She indicated the mud with a wave of her hand.

"One pup survived. Mr. Kenny plastered her in mud and I was attending to her." He didn't like the glint in Emily's eyes, as if she thought he was going soft. His brow arched, and he regained control of the situation. "Kenny needed my help." He left out what he really meant. If he held on tight enough and willed it so, the pup might live.

The straight line of determination on her lips cracked into the start of a smile. She could read his mind the same as when he was a child. But he wasn't a child. Didn't have a child's problems.

She touched his sleeve, and he gazed into eyes tired from too many years of caring for him. "You'll be needing sleep as much as the girl," she said.

Was she insane? He would no more sleep tonight than would Payton. Furthermore, he didn't need Emily dictating his every step. "I can't sleep. I've lost a good man and nearly allowed his house to burn down around his daughter's head. How shall I sleep knowing I failed him so miserably?"

"Wasn't your fault. When, if you don't mind my saying so, sir, will you stop bearing the brunt of responsibility for everyone in your world? God numbers the days for each of us, and it was the end for Miss Whittard's father."

"Don't call me sir. You're like a mother to me, Emily."

"God numbers our days, Jonathan, dearie. God, not man."

What kind of God reached through eternity and snatched an entire family? What kind? It was the same argument he'd had with God when Alithea died. "And the man's wife? And son? What about them?"

"What about them? We all have a time to live and a time to die. You rescued the miss in there. Be thankful it wasn't her time, as well."

As his boot came to rest on the cherrywood bench, he leaned against his knee, his hand massaging the tight muscles along his jaw. Once again, like the little boy Emily Brewster had nursed and loved, he relied on her for comfort and wisdom. He bit down on his lip where the scar never rested but rippled hard against the tip of his tongue. "Will her sight return?"

"Perhaps, in time. She squinted and I'm convinced she saw a bit when we were talking. A fine sign. We'll wait 'til morning before worrying. See how the night plays out. She's from strong stock, like her father."

His face drew tight and he pressed his lip harder. "A little beauty, like her mother."

She pretended to ignore his comment, but he wasn't fooled.

"Yessir. Mind you, could you ask that lazy girl, Clarisse, to fetch a bucket of lukewarm water? I'll be needing more in a bit to keep the sheets wet." Her hands steered him along the steps. "And while we are on the topic of clothes…"

His face curved in an unexpected grin, relaxing his taut muscles at long last. He leaned in intimately and whispered in her ear, "We weren't on the topic of clothes, Emily."

"Ahh, but we are now, Jonathan, lad."

So like her to speak in riddles, his favorite game as a child. Drawing back, he stared in her eyes and noticed the milky-white covering for the first time. She had grown older when he wasn't looking. "Emily, I know you have a point to make." He straightened as if his full stature would force her thoughts out into the open.

"The girl has nothing. One smoke-stained dress and a smattering of undergarments. Her boots are scorched beyond saving. Are you still planning that trip to London?"

He had forgotten all about London. Now seemed rather inappropriate. But Emily's words rang true; the girl must have clothes. She couldn't go traipsing about the halls in nothing but a nightshirt. If all went well and she improved by morning, he would ride out and arrange for the appropriate purchases.

What did one wear to romp with dogs? "You should make a list so I'll know what to purchase."

"You could ask Miss Anne's assistance."

He pictured blond curls dancing around a smiling face—a woman on a mission as purchases piled up in the dress district. "I could."

# Chapter 3

Days turned into a week, and then two, and then a month. Payton could tolerate the confinement no longer. The people at Kent had been more than helpful and kind, but she wasn't accustomed to being smothered with attention, not even when done in charity. "Mrs. Brewster!"

"I'm here. What's all the shouting?"

The woman, never far from Payton's side, lumbered into her bedchamber. "Are you feeling better now?"

Oh, how she longed for a ride in the hills. To be all alone for the first time since her parents' and brother's deaths. "I'm stronger now. Truly, Mrs. Brewster."

"Emily."

"Miss Emily. I need to go outside and feel the sunshine."

"I see no reason against it, dearie."

Hope yelped in the corner, vying for Payton's attention. She crossed the room and drew the wriggling pup into her arms. Her face was quickly washed by Hope's tongue. Disentangling herself from the pup's enthusiastic attentions, she gently placed the puppy back on her blanket.

"Where are the clothes Mr. Lambrick brought?" She had seen Mrs. Brewster with them when first he returned. But where had the woman put them? She gazed about the room. Of course, the wardrobe. With a slight limp—her foot throbbed when she walked—she hobbled over and opened the door; her eyes fell on enough dresses for a dozen girls. "Are these *all* for me?"

"He insisted you be dressed in the best. A lady friend picked them out. As a matter of fact, she—"

"I see. But there's not one dress suitable for the stable. Sooner or later, I will find it necessary to move Hope from this room to the stable." Fingering the gowns, she could tell they had been constructed of the finest silk and softest wools. They would never do for her activities. After a few minutes of exploring, she spotted a modest two-piece gown with a flowing skirt. One she would be able to move easily in. "These will do fine. Have I any shoes?"

"Soft leather boots right here, Miss Payton. Sit down and I'll help you. Your feet are still a might swollen."

She spied a small hole in her stocking and tucked her toes beneath her. "I'm not sure how I will ever repay the kindness Mr. Lambrick has shown me." She tugged at her sleeves.

"You won't be repaying anyone anything, Miss Payton. Mr. Lambrick had great respect for your father. He'll not want you thinking on such matters. You just concentrate on healing." Mrs. Brewster frowned but assisted Payton in wriggling into the serviceable gown. Payton pulled on her boots, then lifted the bottom of her skirt and tucked it into her waistband, which provoked a shocked expression on Mrs. Brewster's face.

"Absolutely not! You are not allowed to leave this room appearing like a madwoman. Mr. Lambrick has guests arriving from London any minute, and he would be most displeased."

Allowed? If she didn't put her foot down immediately, this woman would control her every move. "But, Mrs. Brewster, skirts get in the way."

"A lady *never* dresses like…a man."

How foolhardy. "Well, of course they do. I've done it my entire life."

"It is evident your parents were not slaves to your up-bringing."

Not true. They had taught her compassion. To love when no one else did. Silly things like skirts held no great significance. She glanced into Mrs. Brewster's face, lips pursed so tightly they almost disappeared into her skin. This battle was lost for the moment. She untucked the skirt and smiled. With a quick nod she dashed past the mirror. Her hair. What could be done about her hair? At least it wasn't as badly burned as she had originally thought.

"Have you any combs I could use to restrain these wretched patches of hair?"

"I thought about that. I'll trim the sides and you can pin the back into a coil of curls—of sorts. Then, with a little curl here and there and a suitable bonnet, no one will notice part of your hair has been burned."

"Of course not. No one will notice." She groaned and twirled from her reflection. Her beautiful hair, burned above her shoulders in places. "Well, the fresh air will do me good, even if I look like a crazy woman." She ruffled the hair with wild hands, glanced at the housekeeper and laughed. Happy to feel her joyous self return, she smiled at Mrs. Brewster's raised brow and tight expression.

Autumn leaves crackled beneath her feet and the crisp air filled her senses until her eyes welled and stung. The sun, still too bright for her tender eyes, irritated the skin surrounding them. And with one look in the direction of the cottage ruins, tears flowed openly. In one month she had lost her mother, her father, her brother and her home. She lived with strangers and didn't know how long she could stay before they would expect her to be on her way. Her anger simmered just below the surface but not with the people at Kent Park. At first she had been angry with God, but that lasted as long as the pain from the burns. In her heart she knew better. He had seen her through terrible tragedy and she was grateful for His presence. Perhaps in time all the hurt would heal as her eyes had.

A gust of air blew from the stable and carried the odor of animals, manure and hay. An earthy smell—one she loved. She breathed deeply and grinned; without wasting another second, she moved in that direction.

"Mornin', Miss Payton." Mr. Kenny tipped his warped leather hat and she smiled back, so full of gratitude for his careful tending of Hope. His face, a mirror of compassion, gazed back at her.

"I want to thank you again for looking after Hope, Mr. Kenny. She's so much better now. I have a basket for her with an old piece of soft wool for her comfort. She's happier than Mr. Lambrick is about her residing in the house. I'm not sure he's fond of a yapping pup. Hunter is so calm and gentle…and quiet."

"I'm sure he truly doesn't mind, Miss Payton."

She lifted one brow as she wondered and then realized she didn't care.

"He's a fine gentleman, Miss."

She wanted the puppy with her and that was that. If she were to be imprisoned at Kent, so would Hope. She ignored Mr. Kenny's bowing and scraping at the feet of his master. "Is there any chance of my riding this morning?"

"You ride?"

"Absolutely. Whenever your master's away, one of the stable boys saddles Winter for me. I've been riding her for three years."

He couldn't hide his amusement. "I won't be askin' which boy that was. T'would cause him a mountain of grief with the master, now, wouldn't it? But I can guess."

And her amusement matched his with a smile and shrug of her shoulders. "I do so appreciate it. *If* you think Mr. Lambrick would approve."

He reached for the saddle and headed toward Winter's stall. "I guess we're a bit past worryin' about Mr. Lambrick's approval, now, aren't we?"

She giggled and tucked in her skirt, ignoring the frown so similar to that of Mrs. Brewster. "You'll need the other saddle, Mr. Kenny. I ride astride."

His jaw dropped and she shrugged her shoulders. "Mr. Kenny, is this to be an issue between us?"

"No, miss. I'll fetch the saddle." But his lip and right eye twitched and he mumbled under his breath as he saddled the mare.

As she looped a leg over to straddle Winter's back, she knew she had to set Mr. Kenny straight so there would be no confrontations in the future. "Now don't scold. I always ride this way. I can't imagine how disagreeable it must be to ride with my legs dangling over the side. I might trot a bit, but I could never truly *ride*." She offered her best smile to appease him. "Thank you, Mr. Kenny." Her hand waved as she booted gently on Winter's sides, and the two raced out of the stable as if they belonged together. In fact, they did.

She found she was lost in the beauty of the countryside, fallen leaves a blanket of crunchy, musty beauty from one meadow to the other. One with the horse, jumping, flying, dashing in and out of pastures and through the forest glen. Free. As free as a bird after being caged for a month. Her hair fell loose and she refused to stop and pin it up.

Deep in the woods, she must have been gone an hour before she heard heavy hooves behind her and a loud, commanding voice pulling alongside. "Did Mrs. Brewster give you leave to ride?"

Lambrick grabbed the reins, and her heart leaped in her throat. Caught. Well, she wouldn't behave like a guilty child. She decided when and where she rode. But with the strong touch of his fingers as they grazed hers, she felt nothing like a child.

She swallowed hard. "No one gives me permission to move about. I did ask if I might take Winter out, however. Mr. Kenny agreed." She bit her lip, wondering if he could read the half-truth. "Well, he didn't exactly disagree." Would they never stop treating her like a child? The dark cloud on his forehead foretold of a dressing down. She straightened, head up, chin jutting forward, and plunged on. "I was not aware I was in need of anyone's permission." With a shrug and grunt, she twisted from his glare.

"You could have been hurt. What were you thinking? Your eyes have barely healed. And you are miles from the hall. If you'd fallen…"

She whipped back to face him and noticed for the first time he wasn't riding alone. A lady accompanied him. "I didn't fall. But I am sorry. I assumed if Mr. Kenny said it was all right, it would be fine with you." She watched the scar on his face pulse, his anger evident. And why should she suddenly care that he rode with some lady? "Are you going to introduce me?"

"I shall make introductions at the house. You'll return with us. And why are you riding like a man? Completely inappropriate."

She snatched the reins from his hands, doing her best not to make contact with him, and nudged Winter's sides as she called over her shoulder, "We'll discuss *that* back at the hall, as well."

Standing at the marble fireplace in the great room, Jonathan flicked small specks of wood off his palm into the blaze. Nights had grown colder, and soon there would be fires throughout the house, day and night. He stared as Anne and the rest of his friends strolled into the room. He offered his arm and escorted her to a chair. "You must be tired after the long ride."

"Not terribly. Will your ward be joining us?"

He scowled. Never sure of Payton's whereabouts, he hoped she would make an acceptable entrance soon. "Unless she's seen fit to take her supper with the servants again."

"Oh, Jonathan." She tugged at his arm, rolled her eyes and shook her head. "You must put a stop to that kind of behavior. If she's to be a young lady, you'll have to take charge of her right away before any more peculiar habits set in. I am still dismayed at your allowing her to live here. She must have family."

Addison Barstow lifted a cigar to his nose, sniffed appreciatively and placed it between flaccid lips. He lit the end and chided Jonathan through the smoke. "You know she's right, man. A young lady must adhere to convention." He pulled a scented handkerchief from his pocket and held it to his nose, a sneer barely hidden in his puffy countenance.

Patronizing oaf. "I am aware of what young ladies must do. She needs time. She has lost everyone dear to her. I won't press her so soon. All in good time."

Anne yawned into her hand, stood and rejoined him. She spoke in a barely audible whisper, "There's no one, no one at all who might offer her a home?"

"My solicitor investigated the matter of family members but found no one. Her grandfather's estate was entailed away to a male heir far along the line. Mrs. Brewster will have to do her best."

A gaze that sparked correctness at all costs lowered to him. "Mrs. Brewster isn't a proper woman to bring up a young lady."

He turned back to her as his face warmed. "She raised me, Anne. Have you any complaints about my behavior?"

Her face flamed to match his. It was painfully obvious she was as enamored with him as her sister had been... in the beginning. If truth be told, she had been the one to attract him in the first place, long before he had met Alithea. But he had no plans to respond to her attentions. Not to any woman, ever again.

Sitting before the mirror above her washstand, Payton twisted the strands of hair on either side of her head around her fingers. Most of the burned tresses had been cut away. And with her hair pulled from the back into lovely curls at the sides, her appearance seemed adequate enough. She pinched her cheeks and noticed how bright her eyes appeared now the red was vanishing. Her father had always said they seemed bluer because of her dark brown, almost black, hair. Thick, like her mother's.

Fashionable puffs of silk tickled her shoulders and she fingered the luxurious material. Grown up, even for her. Although she would be one and twenty on her birthday come next April. Then she might make her own decisions. For now, however, she had to stay on at Kent Park with Mr. Lambrick as her guardian.

She wished her heart didn't beat wildly whenever he approached her. She didn't understand her sudden weakness in his presence. She had seen him many times growing up, but he had been distant, a friend of her father, though younger by many years. These new emotions discomfited her, and she wished she had her mother to confide in. She inhaled, long and slow until the resulting sigh pressed against the confines of the gown.

She would never talk with her mother again.

With one last glimpse in the mirror, she picked up the small bag that matched her gown. Her finger curled the last piece of hair at the side, and she rose. She closed the door to her room and moved to the stairwell. Soft leather slippers cushioned her feet as she padded over the Persian runner. The slippers, unlike the boots she'd worn for work most of her life, were pretty. Who had picked out these luxurious clothes? The woman she had seen riding with Mr. Lambrick, perhaps?

Stepping through the hallway, she spied Hunter on the landing. She hurried to his side and knelt down, ruffling his ears. "You'd better move. Someone might trip over you. Come along." By the scruff of the neck she hauled him out of the way. Letting go, she planted a kiss on his head before gliding to the top of the stairs; he whimpered at her side. "There's a dear fellow."

Mr. Lambrick waited for her at the bottom of the steps with his hand extended. Even the scar couldn't intrude upon the handsome face when he smiled. Instantly, perspiration dotted her neck and her heart beat erratically. She patted her hair one more time and pressed her lips together. Drawing in a deep breath, she descended the stairs. Suddenly she looked up, and the smile on Lambrick's face had disappeared.

Jonathan's breath jammed in his throat. He had expected to welcome the child who had fought for her life this past month. Instead, a woman appeared—a woman unequaled in beauty. How had he missed such a pertinent fact? She wasn't thirteen or fourteen. She had to be much older than he'd originally thought.

He tugged at his cravat, felt his gaze turn into a frown and held out an arm while doing his best to appear calm. Then he forced the welcoming smile back.

Payton slipped along the stairs, graceful and quiet, not rowdy and loud as was her nature when she thought no one was looking. Before escorting her into the great room, he skillfully placed her hand on his arm and directed her to where a light repast had been readied.

Anne glided to his side with her fingers clutching his sleeve. "Jonathan, darling. Who is this delightful creature? Perhaps you could introduce us properly, now."

He cleared his throat. "This is Miss Whittard, a friend of the family who has recently come to reside at Kent Hall. Miss Whittard, this is Anne Newbury, sister of my late wife, Alithea." His throat constricted at the mention of Alithea.

Payton opened her mouth, but closed her lips tightly. He released her dainty hand and stared into eyes as blue as the cornflowers Emily placed on the hall table. For a moment, his mind turned from thoughts of Miss Anne Newbury. As if she could read his thoughts, she grasped his arm even tighter.

Payton bowed demurely but never moved her gaze from Anne as Jonathan introduced his guests one by one. Was she considering Anne's role in his life? "I would be pleased if you would call me Payton, Miss Newbury. I am happy at last to have a friend here."

Jonathan cleared the lump from his throat and frowned. "Have we been so harsh with you, Miss Whittard?"

Payton offered him her back and stepped to the fire, where he imagined the light snapping in those blue eyes. "Not at all, sir."

Anne pulled him closer and whispered in his ear, "Don't press her, Jonathan. You are right. She needs time. She's a child, and time shall be her healer. Allow me to fix you a plate. Venison. Your favorite." She raised her voice to unusually loud. "And I believe I see sugared blackberries from your garden. Mrs. Brewster spoils *both* of us, as usual."

Payton turned and stared at Anne.

The evening continued with cards and amusing anecdotes, but too soon Jonathan chose to remove himself from the gaiety. He felt a pain in his heart he didn't understand. These past few years he had worked diligently to remove himself emotionally from the heartache he'd known when Alithea... When she died. He shook his head, clearing cobwebs, and gazed at Anne sitting by his side. Perhaps, more often than was wise, she caused him to remember his dear wife.

No! Alithea was not a dear wife. She had left him for another man. And Anne's face did remind him of her. He pushed her clinging hand away and stood. He had grown to rely on the familiarity, and it not only wasn't fair to him, it was not fair to Anne. She had made it clear long ago, before he'd met Alithea, that she wanted her place at Kent. That would not happen.

Jonathan rose. "If you will all excuse me, I have work to do."

"Oh, Jonathan. Not tonight." Anne, acting like a coquette, batted her eyes. "If you sit, I shall play the pianoforte. I know you cannot resist my music. May I tempt you?"

She tempted him all right but not in a way that pleased him. As a nagging surrogate for Alithea, right down to the blond curls coiled around her ears and the nape of her neck, his heart clawed at him whenever he soaked in her appearance. "Not tonight." Not ever.

With a pout firmly planted on her face, he understood the amusements of the evening were exhausted. "If you'll all excuse me," she said, "I'll retire then." She slipped across the room and covered Payton's hand with hers. "Payton. How nice to have you here, dear child."

Jonathan raised a brow, causing his scar to pull tight across his cheek. He wasn't exactly sure what to make of Anne's sudden interest in Payton.

"Then we shall all retire. My work will wait until morning."

"Would you show me to my *new* room, Jonathan?" Anne smiled at him, but it wasn't really a smile, more of a twisted expression he had never noticed before. She was toying with him. No doubt reprimanding him for giving her usual rooms to Payton.

Payton's face fell in a way that told everyone she felt she was an imposition. She tugged at his heart when she leaned toward Anne and whispered, "Have I taken your room, Miss Anne?"

# Chapter 4

Flames licked about Payton's face, teasing her with sharp, stinging pain. Wood charred her fingers. Her puppy gazed at her and howled long and hard.

Payton awakened drenched in perspiration. As she fully opened her eyes, she threw off the coverlet and panted. Reaching for a glass of water from the stand, she recalled the night her house burned.

Loud and real, screams sounded again and again. This was not a dream. She pulled on her slippers and a shawl and padded quickly into the hall.

Candlelight filled the hallway, and she recognized Mrs. Brewster. "Was that you screaming, Mrs. Brewster?"

"Back to bed. 'Twas just the wind. We hear it howling about the peaks often as winter approaches. You'll no doubt become accustomed to it as we all have, Payton dear. Go back to sleep."

Another candle flickered along the hallway, and Cla-

risse burst upon them. Her hair fluttered about her face
and her eyes were wide and bursting with apprehension.
"Have you heard the screamin', mum? Like an animal in
pain. She's here. She's back at Kent Hall."

"No nonsense, girl. And goodness, hold that candle
steady. We won't be wanting any accidents."

Payton's heart beat so loudly she thought they might
hear. With a hand over her throat, she found the words
difficult to ask. "What are you saying, Clarisse?"

"His late wife walks the dark halls of Kent." She
leaned in whispering. "Because he killed her. Everyone
says so."

Utter quiet fell amidst them. There lay hidden a story
here, to be sure, but what? And how could Payton find
out?

"To bed with you, foolish girl!" Mrs. Brewster yanked
Clarisse's arm. "And I wouldn't be repeating that again.
Mr. Lambrick killed no one. Do you hear?"

"Yes, mum." The girl left for her quarters bobbing and
swaying but continued staring over her shoulder with fear
clearly etched on her pale face.

Payton swallowed hard as another light appeared along
the hall. Lambrick's face, a furrow of concern, peered
through the light. Angry at Payton for leaving her room,
or anxious to find out if she'd been the one in danger?

He bellowed, "Mrs. Brewster! What is all the noise?"

"Sir, I'm quite sure I don't know. Perhaps—"

"Jonathan!" Footsteps sounded from partway down
the stairs. Miss Anne topped the landing. With shaking hands, she handed Mrs. Brewster her candle, then
brushed dirt from her fingers. "Jonathan, did you discover who screamed?"

He frowned. "Where have you been, Anne? Was it
you we heard?"

"No. I ran downstairs to see to the noise and fell."

Payton stepped forward, the corner of her shawl in her hand. "Here." She rubbed at Anne's arm.

"Thank you, Payton, dear." But Payton didn't like the way Anne's gaze narrowed when she said *dear*.

"I found nothing. Who was it, Jonathan?" Anne clutched his arm to her and looked into his eyes.

He brushed her aside as his gaze captured Payton's. "Are you all right?"

"Yessir."

Jonathan's face overshadowed all of them. "I intend to find out who caused this chaos. I'll fetch Kenny and we'll discover who or what is frightening my guests."

Mrs. Brewster led Anne toward her room. "Let's get you into a clean gown. You have dirt all over you."

Payton had barely fallen asleep again when she thought she heard another yell, deep, throaty but abrupt. She jumped up, grabbed her wrap and threw it around herself as she ran for the stairs. At the bottom stood Mr. Lambrick, holding his arm and grasping the rail. He turned to Kenny. "Could you find Emily? Ask her to fetch bandages." He looked up the stairs where Payton stood at the top. "Payton, if you would allow me to lean against you."

"Of course, sir. I'll walk you to your room." Descending, she covered the stairs two at a time as she had seen him do.

He then balanced his weight against her frame and managed to slowly climb the steps. "Humiliated, yet alive. I slipped on the same riser that apparently felled Anne and lost my balance on the butcher table. I fear I wrenched my knee in the process. I shall no doubt have a scar to match my other. I shall look a monster before my life is over, frightening little children."

"Who screamed, Mr. Lambrick?" Her eyes widened.

"The wind, just as Mrs. Brewster said. It as an other-worldly sound when it whistles over the parapets." His eyes suddenly held a tenderness she'd not seen before. "Are you all right?"

"Certainly. It's you we should be concerned with, sir."

As they entered his chamber, she stopped in the doorway. She didn't belong here, but she put aside convention and assisted him to the bed. He sat on the edge. Blood flowed freely from his head and his arm, causing her to be unsure what to do.

He sighed. "I must look a mess."

"No, sir," she mumbled. "You're quite as handsome as ever." Then she gasped and clutched her hand to her chest. How could she have been so bold? What would he think of her? She bit her lip to stop further words and turned her gaze away.

"I'm old, Miss Payton. Not handsome. Old enough to be your—"

"Older brother, perhaps." She couldn't prevent the smile covering her face.

"You're kind, Payton."

"Where is Kenny?" Her fingers brushed the hair from his eyes. "Someone better hurry along with the bandages. You're bleeding."

His hand captured her fingers, warming her palm... and her heart, causing her to babble. "My father was older than my mother. He did not marry her until his own good parents died. His younger brother ran away with... Well, he ran away and left the farm and care of my grandparents to my father. So, my father did not meet my mother until he was well into his years. Nearly two and thirty." She swallowed hard, quelling the rambling that had overtaken her lips.

"You have an uncle, then."

"Father heard not a word from him once he departed. Father said he had no doubt died at sea. But here I am talking about my family and you are suffering from your injuries. What can I do to help you?"

His smile warmed her to the center of her being, and she discovered she couldn't look away when he held out his hand. "Very well. Could you help your *older brother* off with his boots? I am not sure I could remove them with much success in my condition."

In spite of her warming face, she helped to tug the boots off his feet. He eased against the pillows with a groan, and she thought him very pale. "Let me wrap your arm, sir. You are losing a great deal of blood."

His eyes flickered a moment, and he exhaled sharply. She could tell he wasn't used to relying on others. Payton ignored his unwillingness, removed her shawl and tied it tightly around his upper arm. With the end, she blotted at his head until the bleeding subsided. That should do until Mrs. Brewster arrived.

In a matter of minutes, the older woman huffed in. Her arms were filled with dressings and her gaze full of displeasure. Payton should not have entered his chamber alone. She left him to Mrs. Brewster's care and crept back to bed.

In the morning, before the staff had readied breakfast, Anne Newbury and her party of friends had loaded their carriage. "I detest illness. Jonathan may send word when he is well."

Payton stared, afraid to open her mouth and say what she thought. "He may what? Are you leaving now when he needs you most?"

"Dear girl, everyone needs me. I have appointments in London that need my attention. I have overstayed my welcome here. London beckons. And Jonathan has more and better nursemaids here than I." She turned away from Payton and faced Mrs. Brewster. "Tell him I'll await him in London. We shall spend Christmas together as always. Good day, Mrs. Brewster." She offered a chilly salute in Payton's direction and stepped into her carriage.

Without her shawl, Payton shivered against the cold. "Mrs. Brewster, is she actually leaving him to fend for himself?"

"She grows ill at the sight of blood. When her sister died, we, not Miss Anne, cared for the body. She didn't even look at her. People can be queer about such things. If you'll excuse me, Mr. Lambrick is feverish. I should take him a cool drink of water."

"Let me take it, Mrs. Brewster. I'm not skittish near blood. He has been so kind. Let me try and repay his kindness."

She watched the carriage overflowing with trunks and hat boxes drive away and thought how foolish Anne Newbury was to leave such a marvelous man alone.


Lambrick heard a light rapping on his door. He opened his eyes and suffered the stuffiness in the room. Was he dreaming? Heat with the strength of mineral baths closed in on him and his throat constricted. He struggled to remember what had happened. The knocking again.

"Sir? I have water for you."

Annoyed and drained, he shouted, "Come in!"

The door opened carefully. A woman stepped in with a tray of water and tea. She slipped over the shining wooden floor on feet so light he wondered if she were real. "Here, sir. Have some cool water. And I have a cloth for your head. Mrs. Brewster says we need to bring your fever down."

"Who is it?"

"Sir?"

He heard a voice. Whose voice? Alithea? When had Alithea come back to Kent? He looked into eyes blue and thoughtful. A cool hand on his brow. A smell of tea and flowers. His arms reached out of their own accord. He pulled her toward him. Alithea. Warm, young, vibrant and as beautiful as the day he'd met her by the stable... but pushing him away. His grasp tightened about her and he pulled her down, burying his face in her hair. "I've missed you so." He locked his arms and searched for her lips with his own. Soft. She jerked back, freeing herself. The light footsteps slid across the floor as he tried to focus.

"Alithea?" Hot and spent, he fell across the pillows and blew air through his lips and over his damp forehead.

Payton leaned against the wall in the hallway, her heart racing, her fingers touching her mouth. With eyes closed, she felt his lips, pressing soft and warm, then pursuing hers with a vigor she didn't understand. A quiver in her stomach forced her eyes to open wide. Other than a peck on the cheek from her father, she had never experienced a kiss before. But he had thought she was his late wife. Perhaps putting the kiss from her mind and returning downstairs would be prudent.

No matter what, she never would forget that kiss. Never.

"Why, miss, what would you be doin' here? The master call for ya?"

She glanced up and sought Clarisse's kind expression and prayed her face didn't expose the hammering in her chest. "No. I...just took him some water. He was burning with fever. I believe he's getting worse instead of better."

"I'll be tellin' Mrs. Brewster to send for the doctor, miss."

Payton opened the door and tiptoed across the floor; she peered into his room.

"Alithea. It's so hot."

She kept her distance. "It is Payton, sir. Payton Whittard. I am come to bandage your arm."

"Find my wife!" His arms flailed in the air. She froze. His voice rasped with the same dryness she had known after the fire. "Please, God, my wife."

Payton dashed to his side and grasped his arms. "Sir, you must keep your hands still. Your arm, sir. You'll open the wound if you continue thrashing about." With hands deft at healing and words pitched to soothe animals, she pulled the bandage tighter until the opening closed once more and the bleeding stopped. She brushed his forehead and spoke softly so he'd calm himself. Not moving again from his side, she stayed…out of arm's reach.

Would the doctor never come? The wound grew uglier by the hour. Soon, infection would poison his whole body and they would have no choice but to burn it out.

"Hot!" he cried without energy to say more.

With a dog she would know what to do, but a man, a man like Mr. Lambrick, frightened her. "Lie still. I'll summon Mrs. Brewster. Quiet now."

"Don't go. Alithea?"

Should she explain again that she was not his wife? She was no one, just Payton Whittard. So why was her heart aching in her chest, longing to be Alithea for Jonathan? Backing out of the room, in a voice barely louder than a whisper, she answered, "Mrs. Brewster will soon be here, sir."

Was she leaving again? Why, when she had just returned? His eyes blurred as he tried to focus. He licked his lips. Dry. What poisoned his body? His thoughts? They had poisoned him for years. Why didn't Alithea answer him now that she had returned?

Days passed before he could move comfortably in his bed. His lips had cracked and the scar along his face had swollen as if injured anew. Water, not food, was manna to his body. How many days had passed? He struggled to sit up and lean on his elbow, staring into darkness, but he felt weaker than Hope had looked the night of the fire. Carefully removing himself from the bed, he staggered to the window and struggled to haul back the heavy drapes. Light poured through. Squinting, he stared at his body, thin and haggard. He draped his arm over his eyes. Sharp fingers of pain shot through the muscles in his arm and his leg, and his head ached with a lingering throb. He remembered now. He had taken the back stairs toward the scullery and had fallen headlong into a table and then onto the floor. All the table's contents had fallen and a knife had pierced his arm.

Alithea's eyes consumed him. Why was he thinking of her? She had been gone these five years. But he reached for his mouth. She had kissed him, of that he was sure. He fell into the chair by the window, and before a single tear could slide over the stubble on his cheek, he brushed at it and gritted his teeth. Only a dream.

## Chapter 5

Payton could not help gazing as Lambrick leaned against the cane Mrs. Brewster had given him. "Are you all right, sir? You gave us all quite a scare these past few weeks. Fever consumed you and—"

"Find Mrs. Brewster."

"Yessir." She hated to leave him. The servants had begun cleaning for the Christmas ball, a yearly event that Mrs. Brewster told her he had denied himself since Alithea's death. But at Mrs. Brewster's insistence, the ball would proceed. Soon the house would be filled once again with his friends from London and Colchester. And Miss Anne.

How she hoped Anne did not fill his heart. Payton's feelings toward him differed now, though she didn't understand why. Her first month here had been spent mostly in bed, healing from her burns. And then Mr. Lambrick had taken to his bed with fever. She had yet to become acquainted with anyone in the house other than Mrs. Brewster.

"Are you hungry, sir? I would be happy to fetch you a plate. No need to wait for Mrs. Brewster."

"Go away."

What caused the anger? Did he remember the kiss? Was he embarrassed? Though she should be, she wasn't. Her mouth tingled each time she remembered his lips capturing hers in a blaze of heat. Did he somehow blame her? Think she had orchestrated the kiss? No, she wasn't a manipulating female. Would he even know the difference?

She pressed down those thoughts and hurried by the workers in the sitting room, where heavy ropes of garland draped the air in sweet-smelling evergreen. Her nose tingled with the overwhelming odors and she smiled. Though she was safe, this would be a bittersweet Christmas without her family.

Jonathan dropped into a leather chair in the great room, struggling to find a comfortable position. The chair wouldn't help his discomfort. Payton was creeping into his heart, minute by minute, day by day. The odd way she had begun to look at him caused great discomfort. He was too old for all of this folderol. Obviously much younger than he, she deserved something better. He would not condemn her to a life with a man who was an emotional cripple, even if it meant pushing her away before they explored the chasm between them.

And now the ball. How dare Mrs. Brewster go forward while he was abed. No doubt another of her attempts to force him to get on with his life. He'd move on when he was good and ready, not before.

Loud ringing sounded in the hall. "Clarisse, we've

a visitor. Clarisse. Someone!" The girl, no doubt busy stringing red berries across the great hall, did not respond. He forced his feet, one in front of the other, to the door. "Coming."

Clarisse rushed past him with barely a bob of her head, her face red as the berries. "Sorry, sir."

The door grated as it opened to a disheveled man on the stone walk. His features pinched together in an unpleasant attempt at a smile. A few days' growth of beard covered his face and he wore his collar open, improper for any gentleman.

With her hand warily holding the door back, Clarisse waited for the man to speak.

Jonathan pushed ahead, pressing the maidservant aside. "What is your business, sir?"

Nodding, the man stuck out a beefy hand. "Day to ya. The name's Whittard. Edgar Whittard. I hear tell my niece has come to stay at Kent Park. You the manservant or somethin'?"

"Whittard? I was informed her uncle was dead."

"Then you were misinformed. As you see, here I am. Would you be kind enough to call the girl?"

Jonathan reached out. "The name is Jonathan Lambrick. Step inside. We will discuss this in the library."

Whittard gazed from Jonathan's head to his leg, and a smarmy crease dug into his cheeks. "A cripple, eh? Must be difficult with the child underfoot. I were told at the Mug and Ale you had m'brother's girl here. How old is she now? Twelve, thirteen? I come to take her home."

No concern and compassion showed through the sneer, only stained teeth, what there were of them. And the glitter in his eyes turned Jonathan's stomach until his hand clenched. According to Mrs. Brewster, Payton was not thirteen but twenty. "She's not yet one and twenty. I'm her guardian and she shall remain at Kent Park. Her father was a friend of mine and I am committed to her upbringing."

"Her upbringing, eh?" Whittard ran his tongue over his lips. His insinuation hung in the air between them like a heavy, wet quilt.

Jonathan rose to his full stature with great difficulty and he lifted the cane. "Sir?"

Whittard backpedaled, enough so he was out of Jonathan's reach. "Now, I don't mean no harm. But the girl's blood. My responsibility. That's the least I can do for my poor, dead brother and his wife." He clutched a scraggly hat over his heart. "They leave anything?"

So that was what he wanted. Well, let him be disappointed. Unless he was finagling for the last pup, and Payton would never allow Hope to go. "The cottage burned shortly after Miss Whittard moved out. Nothing remains. I can assure you she's being cared for."

"I'd like to see for m'self."

The door opened and a scent of lavender entered, just enough to sweeten the air between them. Payton followed. "Mr. Lambrick."

To Jonathan's dismay, Payton glided across the floor and landed at his side. He cringed at the way her uncle stared. Whittard licked his lips again and stepped toward her, but Jonathan moved more hastily though his battered body cried out.

Jonathan put himself between the two of them. "Go to Mrs. Brewster. She needs you."

"But—"

"Now!" No time for explanations.

"Yessir." Her steps were mere whispers on the floor. She wasted no time, for once, questioning his authority.

Whittard's gaze followed her steps. "She's a lovely

little thing. My missus'll be happy for the extra help. We have five young'uns and she's always tuckered out. Besides, the girl should be with her own family with Christmas so near."

Jonathan lifted a cigar from the box and offered it. "You have interest in the girl or any money she might have coming to her?"

The man's eyes lit up, not unexpectedly. "Money coming to her?"

"Not yet. But we could arrange for a stipend to help ease your pain. Have you come a long way?"

Sweaty hands twisted in front of his odd-shaped body. Short, brindly legs, massive upper arms and a head too small for his stature gave him a menacing appearance, a man Jonathan would not want to come upon in a foreign location. "Long enough. But money ain't the issue. I expect the girl to come with me."

With an aching stride, Jonathan paced now and watched every move Whittard made. "Are you able to show me any reason I should believe you are her uncle?"

Whittard straightened, hands at his sides, clutching against brown wool pants covered in long-journey residue. "I'm the girl's uncle. What do you expect from me? Papers from the king? I intend to take her home. What kind of man are you keeping a young girl from her family? Is she living here alone with you, or do you have a missus?"

Jonathan's breathing labored. Still sick from the previous week, he struggled with more than his injuries; he struggled with the nagging feeling this man's intentions were designed to harm Payton. "She has a houseful of servants for whatever she might need. And I do not care for your implications, Mr. Whittard. I shall call her back in and see if, in fact, she remembers you."

"That won't do no good. She were a wee thing last time I seen her. I stopped at my brother's back then to see if any... To see if he needed any help. But he weren't a friendly sort. Bring her in. I'll wait here while she packs her belongings."

Jonathan's stomach soured and he wasted no more time. "Clarisse, fetch Payton."

The stranger held out his arms in a familiar manner, but the rough-looking man frightened her. Who was he? "Mr. Lambrick?"

Jonathan moved to her side, planting his foot so that his body prevented Whittard's approach, but all the while the contact fluttered from her side to her heart. "Payton, this man has informed me he is your uncle. Do you recognize him?"

This couldn't be her uncle. Her father was a clean man, a good man with a smile that brought joy; this man's smile made her want to run and hide. "I have never met my uncle. My father only said he had a brother who ran away because he and a girl... He ran away. And left father to care for their parents."

"That's a dirty lie! I never run away. They made me go when—"

Lambrick held up his hands. "Perhaps the least said, the better. The fact of the matter is, he wants you to go with him, Payton. Do you wish to leave Kent Park?"

Perhaps Jonathan wanted to be rid of her. But to send her away with that man? Surely not. Nothing short of being escorted from the house would cause her to leave with him. "No, sir. Not unless that is what you want." He couldn't be that callous, could he? This man was pretending to be her uncle. Though he did have the look of her father. Still and all, she would never go willingly.

"Then, it's settled." He glared at the man. "Time for you to go."

Whittard glared at Payton, and she cringed. The way he stared made her hug her arms across her chest. She stepped farther behind Mr. Lambrick and remained silent.

"I'll be gettin' the law to do what it needs and I'll be back. She's not of age and I am her only living kin. In a fortnight or soon after, she'll be goin' with me all right." He tipped his hat. "For now, missy. Don't you worry. I plan to protect you from this man."

Worry? She wasn't worried. She was terrified. She wouldn't go. Couldn't go. His eyes had raked over her body and she was afraid of what it would mean to go with him. "Mr. Lambrick?" Her eyes welled as she waited for his answer.

His arm lifted to protect her. The cane swung close to Whittard's side. "Don't come back if you know what's good for you."

"Your money and position won't keep the girl here. I'll see you in a fortnight or I'm not Edgar Andrew Whittard." He slammed the door behind him.

Payton grasped Lambrick's arm and pressed in, causing him to stumble against a bench. They both landed with a plunk. He smiled as he slowly eased her to her feet.

"I'm sorry, sir. He frightened me."

He guided her toward the door. "We'll take our meal and discuss it."

"Is he able to force me to accompany him as he said?" She simply would not go. That man caused her to tremble deep inside.

"No, Payton. I will not allow it. Let me think on it while you eat."

Without warning, her eyes filled again and she dashed from the room before he could look inside her and know what she was thinking.

The voices rose and fell, depending on who was speaking. After an extravagant dinner that tasted little better than stale bread, Payton hid in the library away from Mr. Lambrick and Mrs. Brewster. Their voices had risen after supper. And it was all her fault. That man. The man who said he was her uncle. Did he want money from Mr. Lambrick? No. He would have said as much. Why did he want to whisk her away from what had become her home?

She strained to hear them talking.

"But she'll not have any say in it. If you'll excuse my saying so, that's not right, sir."

"Would you have him take her? I tell you, I had only to look in his eyes to fathom what was on his mind. Your going ahead with the ball is the perfect answer to our difficulties."

"Oh. I can't believe such foolishness."

"You should have seen his face when he saw her."

What did they mean? Would her uncle hire her out as a servant? Perhaps that was why he had stared. To see if she was strong and healthy. No. Mr. Lambrick had more than anger in his voice; he had a restlessness. She felt it with every word.

"I tell you, Emily. The man can't be trusted. I can think of no other way to protect her."

"Are you going to speak with Payton or shall I, dearie?"

"Send her to the library. I'll offer her my protection and allow her to choose. After all, she may decide she would rather be with her family, but I pray not."

*No. Not with my uncle. I want to stay here...with Mr. Lambrick.*

"What will this mean for her, sir?"

"Nothing. She will continue to live here under my protection, *nothing* more."

"Nothing?"

In such a short time Jonathan Lambrick had grown to be more than her protector. He filled every corner of her heart. But he mustn't know that.

"Nothing!" he bellowed.

Payton slipped from the library where she had been eavesdropping and tripped over her feet dashing for the sitting room where the downstairs maid dusted decorations. "May I help you, Clarisse?"

"My, there's a storm breakin' around here, now, isn't there, miss? Did you know that man who come?"

"No. I've never seen him before. Here." She lifted the box of decorations for the young maidservant. "I only know he made my skin crawl like spiders dancing on my arms. He looked funny at me."

Clarisse reached for the box. "I seen men look like that before, miss. Like the one who eyes me whenever I go for vegetables for Mrs. Brewster. You'll be wantin' to stay away from him."

Payton shivered and hugged herself again, but it didn't help. "I may not have a choice. He said he was my next of kin. But I thought Mr. Lambrick was my guardian. I don't understand. I don't need *any* guardian."

"Talk to the master first. Don't be worryin' until you know all the particulars." She stretched out her hand and patted Payton's arm. "There now, let the master have his say before you go fearin' things out of your control."

"Thank you, Clarisse. You've been kind to me ever since I arrived. If I must leave, you shall be missed. Everyone at Kent shall be missed. I've grown quite accustomed to you all." Had she said *all* a little too familiarly?

She lifted one of the delicate ornaments from the box, removed the paper and handed it off.

"And we would miss you, miss." Her smile warmed until Payton felt a tad better.

Mrs. Brewster entered, clearing her throat. "Payton, dear, Mr. Lambrick would like to speak with you in the library." She had tears in her eyes, and Payton was afraid he was going to tell her to pack her bag.

Payton's hands shook, and her feet barely scuffled into the room. She looked helpless, so young. Tears filled her eyes before he even spoke to her. Had she heard them arguing? He stood and gestured to the chair by the fire. "Payton, did you hear us talking? Do you know what I want to speak with you about?"

"No, sir. Yes, sir, I mean. Is it about the man who said he was my uncle?"

"Yes. He is going to return soon and he says he will have proof he is your uncle."

"I...I don't wish to leave Kent Park. If you will allow me to stay."

He took in the round eyes that tugged at his every emotion and wondered just how she would feel about his suggestion. And though he had promised himself never again, this was different. He had no choice. One look at her and he understood his duty. "It is possible the law may be on his side, Payton. You are not yet one and twenty. For a year, possibly more, he may be able to keep you with him." His throat felt paralyzed with the thought of what Whittard might do to her, but he tried to remain calm for her sake.

She rose and held her hands to the fire. "But why? What does he want with me?"

What indeed? If only he knew he might be able to pro-

tect her by some other means. But there was little time
and they must take action now or the girl would be lost
forever. "Payton, I don't believe he intends to be honorable where you are concerned. Do you understand what
that means?"

"No, sir." She turned to face him fully and she tried
to smile, but instead her lip trembled and she shook as
one lost in the cold without cape or gloves.

He had no intention of engaging in a parental discussion. Mrs. Brewster would handle that part. "There
is no way for me to keep him from you save one. If you
are in agreement, of course." He took her hands in his.
So small and helpless. His stomach churned to think of
that man's paws on her. "Does any of this make sense,
Payton?" Her grasp, cold and frightened, had begun to
thaw his heart.

"You look so stern, Mr. Lambrick. Did I do something to anger you?"

"No. You did nothing wrong. Sit back down. Please."
With a lack of care, he moved too quickly and pain racked
him. He sucked in a breath that tore through his body like
fire. She turned toward him and rose again.

"Are you all right, Mr. Lambrick?"

"Payton, I have to say this, no matter how incredible
it may sound. Mrs. Brewster and I have no other solution
to offer. Payton, if you will marry me, your uncle cannot
take you away. Do you understand?"

"Marry you?"

The look on her face, as if she had just been offered a
glass of vinegar instead of wine, a sow instead of a kitten. "Listen. He would not be allowed to force you from
Kent Park." He stared at the cane and sighed. "I understand I'm not much to look at, but it's me or old Mr.
Kenny or Birdie. You may say no and I will understand."

He fingered the scar that stretched down his cheek and thought how hideous he must appear to a young woman. Aware that the women he knew tended to attach themselves more to his purse than his looks, he had no idea what she might say.

They both remained quiet for what seemed an eternity. Was that a tentative smile or fear that crossed her features? If only... But he mustn't allow personal feelings to enter into this arrangement in spite of the way she had begun to inch into his heart.

"I will abide by your decision for me, sir. All of you have been kindness itself, and if you believe me in danger, I will do as you say. But what about Miss Anne? I thought there was—"

"Nothing between us." He understood Anne, all right. She was first in line for the money. Anything to restore her precious Newbury. She had made that clear years ago. Before Alithea. "We are friends. That is the only understanding between us." He glanced away. "I know I have little to offer."

"Mr. Lambrick, you are the handsomest man I have ever known." She blushed, stepped back and bit the edge of her lip. "I suppose I sound forward. I am sorry." He laughed and she turned back to look him in the eyes. "I have never heard you laugh before."

"No?"

"You should do it more." She smiled and her arms reached out, but he pinned them to her sides.

"This will be nothing more than a marriage for your safety. I intend to keep him from harming you. That's all. Are you in agreement?"

Without pause she stepped back, and he didn't miss the pain that overcame her face. "Of course. I never thought you meant—"

But she had. He could tell. "We must make every-one believe we are in earnest. We should exchange our vows the night of the ball. I'll arrange for the special license, and we'll wed at midnight. Surprise all of the guests. With Mrs. Brewster's help, could you be ready?" She should at least be allowed a wedding. Friends and a feast. The Christmas ball would provide the perfect set-ting. "Well? We've barely a fortnight to prepare. Will that do? Answer me, Payton. We have little time if you are to be missish."

Her jaw rammed forward in a way he'd grown famil-iar with. "I will be ready."

"Tomorrow I'll send Birdie to town and have Miss Anne purchase a gown. A very pretty gown."

"There's no need, sir."

"Perhaps you should call me Jonathan. If we are to be believed."

"Very well…Jonathan."

"And you shall have a gown. The most beautiful gown in all of London."

# Chapter 6

With Clarisse, Payton toured the greenhouse and snipped enough flowers to fill the great ballroom. Though the wedding would be a sham, Payton's excitement stirred in her breast. She had grown to love Jonathan Lambrick, ever since he'd kissed her. But, of course, that must remain her secret. His kindness should not be mistaken for love. He had been clear—this was a marriage of convenience to protect her from her uncle. She quivered whenever she thought of her uncle staring at her and was grateful Jonathan had thought of a way to provide shelter. *Oh, God, am I doing the right thing? You said in Psalms You were my Protector, but is this the way? I know my father respected Mr. Lambrick—Jonathan.*

They filled the baskets and skipped over the thick path of straw that had been put down to prevent a muddy walk the night of the ball. Payton shooed Clarisse ahead, and she stopped momentarily to visit with Mr. Kenny. She remained ever grateful to him for saving her puppy. As he fed Storm, she couldn't resist offering half an apple to the magnificent animal.

"I do thank you for Hope."

"There's no need, Miss Payton."

She pulled a flower from the basket and tucked it onto Mr. Kenny's shirt. "There now. You're all ready for the…ball."

He winked at her. "I know what we'll be a celebratin'. Congratulations to ya."

"Does everyone know our secret?" She smiled before turning toward the entrance.

After warming by the fire, Clarisse nodded with her hands on her hips. "We've a sight of work to do." She crawled up a ladder. "Could you pass the red berries up? I think I'll weave 'em into the greenery. They should look nice and colorful, with tiny little candles lit just before the vicar arrives. Oh, how lovely 'twill be."

Payton's heart was so full, she hardly understood the feelings. But her gratitude could barely be expressed. She simply said, "Thank you, Clarisse." Would she always feel closer to the help than to Jonathan? If only he looked at her the way her father had looked at her mother. Her arms would pull him to her. No, he had said he was marrying her to protect her from her uncle. Only to protect her.

Clarisse's face beamed. Had Alithea taken time to thank the help? She wished she knew more about the woman. "By the way, a box arrived for ya. I saw Mrs. Brewster lug it upstairs. Yer gown?"

Payton's eyes widened, and she grinned before she could stop herself. "If you don't mind, I'll go see." She loosened her skirt from the waistband lest someone catch her, and she dashed for the stairs. Rounding the top, nearly out of breath, Jonathan startled her.

"Your skirt appears wrinkled. Has Clarisse forgotten to press it for you or have you been—"

Caught. And she wouldn't allow Clarisse to accept the blame just to save her hide. She did her best to quiet her breathing. "No, sir. I left it on a chair last night and Hunter must have slept on it." Not exactly a lie. She *had* left it on the chair and he *might* have slept on it.

"Shame on Hunter." He laughed a deep, low rumble from his throat. "You would let the poor animal be blamed for your disgraceful behavior? Shame on you, Payton Whittard. And my name is Jonathan, not Sir."

His taunting gaze let her know he forgave her for the bad habit of hiking her skirt. "Yes, Sir Jonathan." She giggled before pushing wide her door and then slamming it behind her. Her heart fluttered and her breath steadied shakily as she recalled his laughter. Such a wonderful sound.

On the bed, a creamy silk gown with a light blue shimmer lay between two sheets. She ran her fingers over the silk and a gasp caught in her throat. She had never owned anything so beautiful. A slim box lay next to the gown. She opened it and squealed with delight. Three strands of braided pearls with a diamond-studded clasp nestled in the velvet lining. She appreciated he was doing all he could to make her happy, even if the marriage was... not to be real. She sighed. She would be safe. More than that, she could stay at her beloved Kent Park with all of her friends.

Her legs dangled over the edge of the bed. Kid leather slippers with cream-colored ribbons would peek under her gown and all the women would be envious. She would say "I do" and they would faint. Jonathan was so hand-

some. She would be wealthy. She had never thought of
that before. And they would entertain and go to London. In a matter of seconds, her smile was replaced
with a frown. She would have all of these *things,* but she
wouldn't really have a husband. Moving to the chair in
front of her vanity, she dropped down and noticed another gift. A silver comb she recognized as her mother's.

She opened the door and caught Jonathan leaning
against the wall. He grimaced slightly, and gazed in her
direction, his face a mixture of amusement, impatience
and pain. "Well? What do you think? Will the ladies be
envious?"

He had no inkling how envious. "Yes, of course. And
Mother's comb. Thank you. Where did you find it?"

He shouldered through the doorway. "In the ashes. It
seemed to have come through the fire quite well once
Clarisse scrubbed it." His hint of a smile nearly choked
her. "Is the gown to your liking?"

"It is beautiful. I shall never be able to thank you properly." *Although I wish I could thank you, very well indeed.* She stared at the chiseled shape of his mouth and
her cheeks grew warm.

"There is a veil, which Mrs. Brewster will keep hidden until the stroke of twelve."

Her smile could be confined no longer and she clapped
her hands, like a foolish child on Christmas morning. "I
am so very happy, Mr. Lambrick. You have been as kind
to me as my own father."

"Your father!" His face darkened. He said not another
word, but left the room. The heavy footsteps on the stairs
told of his displeasure.

Anne Newbury and a party of five arrived with great
fanfare two days before the ball. Jonathan was nowhere

to be seen, so Payton welcomed Anne, trunks, boxes and all. She tried her best to act the lady and forget how unkind Anne had been to Jonathan when last she was at Kent Hall. "Thank you, Anne. Your being here means a great deal to Jonathan."

"It's 'Jonathan' now?" She stepped away from her group and whispered in Payton's ear. "You sly little thing. I've been away such a short time and already you have him panting at your side. So it's innocence he longs for?"

Anne rejoined her party and smiled broadly, leaving Payton to guess at her meaning. Payton did her best to understand what had happened between Miss Anne and Jonathan after his wife's death. At times, she thought they had once been a couple, but she couldn't be certain. Did Jonathan not see how Anne longed to be part of his life?

When Anne drew to Payton's side again, she said, "Miss Whittard, I would like you to meet my cousin, Addison Barstow, his sister, Caroline Brayden, and her husband, Edward. This handsome fellow is Wallace Fitzhugh, an old beau of my sister's. He's a foe of Jonathan's but we shall be discreet. What say you, Wallace?"

"I say, where is the old boy? I haven't laid eyes on Jonathan since he wed Alithea. I have no doubt he remembers that encounter very well."

"Why is that, Mr. Fitzhugh?" Payton asked, unsure she wanted the answer from the mysterious expression on his face.

"We had a nasty brawl when he discovered me showering his bride with kisses."

She gasped and Anne reached for her hand. "Darling, they have no doubt long since given over their hard feelings. Wallace and Jonathan grew up boyhood friends, and I just knew Jonathan would not want a wedding without him here."

So the wedding was only a surprise to the locals? Naturally if Anne had arranged for her gown, she might have told the others. She blinked. What exactly was Anne planning?

Just then Jonathan breezed through with a hearty welcome. "Did I hear you say *wedding?* Who let the cat out of the bag?" His eyes opened wide when he observed Wallace Fitzhugh standing behind an assortment of satchels and trunks. A hat box in Wallace's hand prevented him from shaking hands with his boyhood friend.

Payton could not politely look away but instead stared at the men, wondering at their history.

Fitzhugh sneered. "You look well, Lambrick. I'd not have known you had Anne not pointed you out. Still the handsome rake, I see."

Jonathan scowled but offered a slight bow, enough to be polite. "And how is it you accompanied Anne?"

Payton sensed the tension building and wished to do or say something to pacify the two stags pawing at the ground. "Anne prevailed upon your childhood companion to escort her. Wasn't that thoughtful, Jonathan?"

"Very." He slowly moved to Payton's side. Tenderly lifting her hand, he kissed her fingertips as he smiled. "Have you met my fiancée, Wallace? Payton Whittard."

"Yes, we met. A lovely girl. I'm envious."

"You always were." Jonathan's eyes sparkled with more than humor, and Payton stepped back, the air so thick with words unsaid, she was suffocating.

She tugged at Jonathan's arm and moved them all toward the great hall. "Would you care for some light refreshments after your long journey? Mrs. Brewster has had the cook prepare many of Jonathan's favorites for you. If you'll be kind enough to follow me." She grasped his arm tighter and directed him away from

Wallace Fitzhugh. Already, she did not care for or understand this connection.

He leaned down and whispered in her ear, "Thank you. But Payton, understand this, even when injured I still am able to fight my own battles." Then he smiled, no doubt for his guests' sake. She noticed Anne providing them a side glance, and she returned the look. Smiling at Jonathan came easily and she would be happy to do it more often than merely for show.

She whispered back, "I shall remember, Sir Jonathan."

He swatted at her hand with a frown. Hunter trotted after them and lay at Lambrick's feet when, at last, he eased into his leather chair. He patted the seat next to him as if implying ownership. Well, she was no one's property.

Instead, she turned to her guests. "Jonathan said you love berries, Miss Anne. I had cook prepare them special with a dollop of cream, cinnamon and honey. And never fear, they were picked last summer and dried. Would you care for a dish?" She offered the cut-glass bowl as if she knew what she was doing. She didn't. But no one else had to know. She glanced at Jonathan. Was he pleased?

"Darling, how sweet of you. And my favorites—blackberries. You are too kind." She lifted her brow, perhaps asking Payton if they were engaging in cat and mouse.

Was Payton imagining mischief at work? She would take care around Anne until she figured the older woman out. For now, she played mistress of Kent Hall and she would behave accordingly, like some remarkable actress in one of Molière's works.

"Thank you for arranging for my gown. It's splendid."

Anne drew Payton aside. "I wanted it to be perfect, and I remember how much Jonathan loved Alithea in the palest blue. Her eyes were brilliant when she wore blue. I hope you'll have a similar reaction from him."

As if a horse had kicked her in the gut, Payton staggered back and came to rest at Jonathan's side. He reached out. "Payton?"

"I am fine. Would you like me to get you a glass of wine?"

The scowl again and she stepped away. "I'm bruised, Payton. I'm not a cripple. And no, I don't drink wine."

"I didn't mean to imply—" She wasn't sure what she had meant, but he had taken it as an insult to his manhood. This Fitzhugh character had unsettled Jonathan more than she'd realized. If only she might help him. She longed to clear the sadness from his heart.

His frown quickly replaced with a smile, Jonathan's voice rose with an odd familiarity, or did she imagine his attention toward the ladies? "Caroline, could you play the pianoforte when you finish your crepes? I haven't heard you play in a very long time." He leaned toward Payton. "She is the finest pianist I have had the pleasure of listening to."

Hope sank in her. Here she sat next to Jonathan but his mind consistently wandered to Caroline, then Anne, then... Oh, why had jealousy suddenly snared her heart?

How could he play this game? He had to convince his guests of his sincerity, yet he couldn't hurt Payton by leading her on, allowing her to think their bargain rang true. He should distance himself from her unless absolutely necessary. With effort, he walked to the pianoforte and began a conversation with Caroline.

Before long, Anne sidled to his side. She stroked his hand and whispered in his ear, "How is the arm, now, darling? That was a nasty fall you took when I was here."

"I'm better, thank you." He turned away, putting an end to her fawning. "Caroline, could you play my favorite? Do you remember?" As she began to play, he laughed. "Yes, of course you do." He glanced toward Payton to see if she watched him with the ladies. She had to understand their arrangement. A small hurt now would be better than a misunderstanding later. And the more they were together, the more he realized how difficult this game would be. One minute he longed to protect her, pet her, care for her, and the next he felt the need to keep her safe by keeping his distance. His head ached with the conflicting messages swirling through his mind.

Caroline blushed. "Still a terrible flirt, aren't you Jonathan?"

He looked at the hurt on Payton's face. If only it were that simple.

They wouldn't miss her. Payton stepped first into the hall, and when no one noticed her leaving, she fled up the long, winding stairs. On the landing, she tried to seek out Hunter, but the traitor must have remained with his master in the great hall. What was the painful empty space in her heart? Did Jonathan expect her to live with him all the while he gave his attention to other women? Didn't he see how she longed for him to love her? Her eyes filled with tears even before she opened her door. As her hand reached out, another hand, larger and warmer, closed over the top.

"Did you think I wouldn't notice your departure?"

She sniffled and aimed her line of vision away from him. "You were busy, sir. I understand. Miss Anne is beautiful. As is Miss Caroline. We have no special agreement. I realize why you are marrying me, and while I'm grateful, I have not fooled myself into believing this is any more than a convenience done for my welfare. For you, I'm not sure what it all means. If you will excuse me, I'm rather tired." Her shoulders sagged and she wished she could face him with courage, but tonight had drained her of her confidence.

"Everyone but Anne believes this marriage is real. And it has to look to the world as if we are in love."

She spun back as fire flushed her face. "In love! How will they believe that when you are fawning over every woman in the room? Will they truly believe we are in love, sir?"

His hand dug into her arm, and he pulled her close to face him. His eyes took her in, searched her heart.

Her breath hitched as he forced her closer. "If we don't convince the others... If we don't marry tonight, your uncle may do whatever he wishes with you until you are one and twenty, and perhaps beyond. That is what is at stake, Payton. We must be actors a while longer. No one must know you have any living relative. And since you have reason to think my thespian talents lacking, I assure you, from this moment on, I shall be the epitome of one of Shakespeare's actors. You want an ardent lover and I have an obligation to keep you safe." His arm drew about her, completely releasing her grasp on the wall until he had her firmly in his arms.

She tried to free herself, but his grip tightened like iron. His head dipped forward until the sweetness of his breath mingled with hers. His gaze bore into her in a way that said not to disobey—he worked for her best interest. His lips continued to linger above hers until her heart raced and her eyes darted from side to side, so afraid was she to give away how she felt. Mere seconds passed as his embrace entrapped her. The closeness and warmth from his mouth frightened her in a strange, not wholly unpleasant way. His breathing was faster and his eyes were glazed; all the time he never looked away. Was he telling her that he cared? Truly cared?

"Jonathan?"

"Payton. Why can't you just…" His lips fell across hers like silk petals. She tasted his strength for the first time. A pounding behind her ribs awakened her to his nearness. He did care in spite of how he acted in front of the others. He cared! In no time, her own mouth betrayed her as she wrapped her arms about his waist and returned his kiss.

A gasp caught in her throat as he released her with a gentle push. She stumbled back, hand on her chest.

His eyes flashed with what? Anger? What had she done now? "Go to bed, Payton. But tomorrow you need stay right by my side while we entertain. My eyes will be on no one but you. Do you remember what is at stake?"

She nodded, numb to her toes. What did he expect from her? She would not be a toy, a foolish girl with no feelings of her own. But what exactly was she feeling? "I'll not forget. I am fully aware of my obligation for your help. Good night, Mr. Lambrick."

Jonathan had to take care. This act, essential to her benefit, was finding him the court jester. He stammered when he spoke with her, his legs weakened while his arms ached to hold her as closely as humanly possible. His lips longed to crush hers. But he had to take care not to let that happen again. He could not love her and she could not love him. So, why had he suddenly kissed her, felt her as much a part of him as his own body? He stood at the door and heard her crying. He should dash propriety to the wind and go to her. Tell her how his feelings had changed. But then he would be at her mercy as he had been first at Anne's until he understood she wanted only his money, and then at Alithea's, a woman who wanted every man who paid her attention.

Tension filled him, and he walked to the stairs, the muscle sawing in his jaw. He slapped a fist into his palm. She would not find her way into his heart. No woman would. Ever again.

Without thinking, he cast the cane he had grown to rely on over the railing and sent it skittering across the entrance. He let out a groan meant for no one's ears. But when he glanced down, he observed Anne standing at the bottom, smiling at his tantrum while Duncan scurried to retrieve the cane.

More tears and Payton wasn't sure why. What was it about him that crept into her very being, tugging at her heart and causing her to cry? She had been robust her entire life. Strong enough to work like a man and still take the time to remember she was a lady. Why, now, did this man affect her so? He had kissed her. His sweet breath had warmed her face. Worse yet, she had kissed him back. Alone in her room, sprawled across her bed and snuggled under the quilt, her eyes closed, but her mind continued its dangerous game of why and what if.

She heard the gongs of the longcase clock on the landing. Midnight. Would she never sleep? At last, with prayers finished a second time, her breathing steadied and her arms and legs relaxed. Hopefully tomorrow would be a brighter day. She sighed deeply.

A loud crash and screams so real they seemed to be coming from her room jerked her awake. She shot up in bed, threw off the delicate coverlet, held a hand to her throat and listened for more noise. Nothing. Had she been

dreaming? She slipped from the bed and donned a dressing gown but gave no regard to slippers.

After unlocking and throwing wide the heavy door,
she held her breath. Hard hands gripped her wrists, pulling them together in one iron grasp. Before she could
scream, one hand shifted and covered her mouth. A voice,
firm and anxious, remained low. "Are you safe?"

Without looking but recognizing the tone, she fell into
Jonathan's strong arms and her head came to rest under
his chin. She tried to speak; no words came forth. He
stroked her hair to quell the shaking. "Shh," he whispered, his words ruffling her hair. "Everything will be
fine. Then it wasn't you?"

"No. But who?"

"I haven't any idea." His fingers smoothed the sleeves
of her gown in comfort, and she softened to his touch. She
pressed into the protection of his embrace. "I wanted to
be assured you were safe before investigating." He leaned
back and looked tenderly in her eyes, but his expression
changed in a blink from compassion to anger. "Go back
to your room. Lock the door. And stay there, Payton!"


Someone was going to great lengths to frighten his
guests and Jonathan would know who before the night
was over. Taking more care this time, he climbed the back
way down the stone steps that would take him through the
scullery and empty near the stable. He passed the kitchen,
where Anne, Mrs. Brewster and two of the servants waited
with candles. "What are you doing here, Anne?"

Anne reached for his arm, boldly stroking the fabric of
his gown, her eyes and mouth round with wonder. "I heard
the screams, Jonathan. Be careful. Alithea's not dead."

"Don't behave like a fool, Anne." He plucked her hand

away in disgust. "I saw her. You saw her. We buried Alithea. She's gone."

She drew closer as he tried to walk away. "But that was her scream, her voice. I would know it anywhere. Oh, Jonathan, hold me."

"Please, Anne." He pushed her gently away. What might have been. He'd courted Anne long before Alithea, and at one time... But that was long ago. He had married her sister.

Turning toward Mrs. Brewster, he asked, "Has anyone left the house for any reason this evening?"

Curls bobbed under her cap and her plump cheeks lacked their usual rosy tint. Instead, her face paled at his words. "No one that I know of, sir. We'd all been sleeping. I came in here when I heard Miss Anne putting on a kettle. I offered to fix her some bread and fresh butter to calm her nerves, but she said she was fine so I returned to my room to get dressed. Then I heard the screaming. I came out soon as I could. Why?"

He wasn't certain. But the door at the back had scraped the floor with mud as if someone had been out and returned. He looked down at the feet of those in the room. All wearing boots or slippers of some sort. "Has anyone checked the stables?"

"Mr. Kenny is there, sir. He said he would sleep with the mare as she's about to foal. He would have seen anyone snooping about. Would you like me to send Birdie out, Mr. Lambrick?"

"No, Emily. Let him sleep. We'll form a party in the morning and see if any mischief has occurred."

Anne maneuvered her way back to his side. Her hands started their clingy caress once again. "What are you thinking, Jonathan?"

He hesitated. After scrutinizing each of them one more

time, he sat with her at the table. "There is the possibility of the girl's uncle."

"Her uncle? You said she had no other family. Jonathan, what game are you playing here?"

"A man showed up at the door claiming to be her uncle. I have no reason to believe he is, but with the other strange occurrences, I have to consider he might be responsible for our nightly screams. As of yet, we have found no reason why Whittard's cottage burned. I am afraid someone may mean to do harm to Kent Hall and all of its properties."

"Why would he want to harm you or this lovely old building?"

"That is a very good question, Anne. Here, take some tea and calm yourself."

While the others choked down cups of tea and wedges of pumpernickel bread, Jonathan thought through all that happened. He rose with every intention of seeing to Payton.

"Talk with Mrs. Brewster and finish your tea. I'm going to check on Payton."

She offered a smile that reached no further than her pouty lips. "Of course. Payton."

## Chapter 7

Payton awoke with a start. Sun filtered tiny fingers around the edges of the curtains as morning welcomed her. It took but a minute to realize the frightening night was over.

None of it had been a dream. The screaming, the fear. His late-night rap on the door to confirm she was safe. His arms securely wrapped around her. She tried but could not stop her smile from spreading. He had come back after checking with Kenny and stayed with her until she grew drowsy. Until she was able to forget the fright. Jonathan Lambrick was a mystery. One minute holding her, the next telling her to get away from him. With a clearing shake of her head, she rubbed her eyes and began a thorough search of the room.

A large white box tied up with a huge, red bow sat at the bottom of her bed. She scrambled over the cover like a kitten after a ball of string and lifted a slip of paper from beneath the ribbon.

*Payton*
*I realize our marriage is for your safety only, but*
*every bride is entitled to a gift. I had intended*
*to give you this for Christmas, but I thought,*
*perhaps, you would laugh and not worry about*
*what happened last night once you see what is*
*in the box.*
*Jonathan*

She tugged at the ribbon until it fell softly into her hand. Her fingers caressed the raised label from a well-known men's shop in London, beautiful enough to frame. With a swift stroke, she removed the top.

Payton gasped. Then she let out a whoop of delight.

Inside lay a cap, a jacket of kid leather and a pair of loose breeches, much like a man's in the same butter-soft kid. Her fingers slid over the clothes until she laughed out loud. Another note lay underneath the last piece of clothing.

*I think I heard your laugh before you even in-*
*spected the contents. You no longer have an ex-*
*cuse to hike your skirt into your waistband. You*
*may feel free to ride in breeches. Only on our*
*property. No one else will know. Your secret is*
*safe with me.*
*Jonathan*

Still bubbling with merriment, she sat on the edge of the bed. Caressing the clothes with her gaze, she realized how much trouble he must have gone to in order to secure these for her. She blinked back tears. Why shouldn't she care for him? He was all kindness itself. Gruff, but considerate. And tomorrow night she would become Mrs.

Jonathan Michael Lambrick. What would that mean for her? Should she live like a spinster the rest of her life? Or someday would this life offer her pleasure, the type of loving, kind marriage her parents had enjoyed? *Father, only You can lead us in the right direction, but know this; I want the kind of love my parents had. And with You, all things are possible.*

The ladies had assembled downstairs already. She could hear them but didn't care. She lifted the jacket and smoothed her hand over the soft material. Before she faced anyone, she would ride. It would be scandalous if they discovered her, but still she pinned her hair up and secured it under the hat. Then, she donned the jacket, breeches and the boots he had bought her soon after the fire. There, the reflection of a young boy met her in the mirror. What fun this would be to come and go without anyone's knowledge of her whereabouts except, perhaps, Mr. Kenny or Birdie. And from experience, she knew they could keep a secret.

Addison, Edward and Wallace lagged behind Jonathan and Storm. His horse wasn't inclined to stay in step with another. They had searched the properties of Kent Park and uncovered nothing out of the ordinary. Who had an interest in persuading people to think Kent Hall had an intruder? An otherworldly intruder?

As Jonathan shifted in the saddle to say as much to Addison, his horse reared, shooting pain through his knee. A rider soared past him, and from the quick glance, he didn't recognize the boy or the horse. He kicked Storm's sides and plunged after him, leaving the others trailing behind.

"You there, stop!" The other horse was no match for

Storm. In less time than it took for Storm to completely stop, he leaped from the animal, landing on the boy and tackling him to the ground.

They tumbled in a heap with Lambrick firmly planted on top of him. He wrestled the hat off and stared into blue eyes. "Payton?"

"Yes, Payton. Now get off me!"

Before moving, he thought how pleasant it might be to stay right where he was if he were to lean down and kiss the sauciness away. He threw his head back and laughed. "I should have recognized you in those clothes."

The men had arrived seconds later and stared, but he didn't care.

Edward leaned forward on his mount. "Who might this be?"

"This, my good fellows, is my very-soon-to-be bride." He untangled himself from legs and arms and hauled Payton to her feet. "Sorry, m'love. I had no choice but to expose your identity." With a hasty move, he plopped the hat back on her head, but her hair tumbled around it in disarray. He turned her and brushed dirt from her billowing breeches until she yanked his hand away.

"I'll do that myself."

Addison spoke through pursed lips, staring openly at Payton's unusual attire. "I do believe the kitten has claws, Jonathan. I wouldn't turn my back in the night."

Jonathan hoisted a blushing Payton back into the saddle, and she immediately rode off. He remounted Storm and pulled the bit away from the others, guiding the animal in the direction of the flying white horse and the lady.

He cracked Edward's horse lightly with his whip and nudged his heels into his mount. "Don't wait breakfast, gentlemen. I've a poacher to overtake."

* * *

Wind whistled through the leathers on Winter, but Payton couldn't encourage her to slow at all, not that she wanted her to. Payton needed to escape. They had both been anxious for this excursion. She yanked hard at the bit, but to no avail. Winter's plan of action was preset and Payton had no choice but to follow.

While leaving the stable, she had been careful to avoid seeing anyone other than Birdie, so it took her by surprise when she heard hooves gaining on her. How imprudent to have been found by an entire party of men and wrestled to the ground like a street brawler.

She wasn't about to allow Jonathan to manhandle her so. In an instant, she realized how prideful she had become since living at Kent. Any other time and she would have been grateful for the kind attention, but Jonathan frightened her. The way he looked at her. When he held her, the way his chin came to rest, warm and inviting, in her hair. He said her name and made it sound like dripping honey. If only he truly cared for her, she would gladly allow him inside her heart, her life, even her soul.

As Winter dashed over the land, Payton's mind returned to the screaming last night, and suddenly another horse was upon her again. With a wrenching motion, she turned hard to see who it was, but she slipped sideways in the saddle. Winter balked and Payton flew off the side, landing on soft ground.

Jonathan remained seated and stared as she squirmed on the ground with her lip curled, brushing at the new clothes. "Well? Are you just going to sit there?"

"I see you have found good use for the protective clothing two times in one day."

"No thanks to you." She shook her head and refused to meet his gaze.

"Me? I didn't throw you off. You landed there through no help of mine."

She felt her face flame red-hot. How dare he speak to her so?

"Have you enjoyed your ride?"

She finally looked up to see him having trouble hiding a grin. "I wouldn't laugh so much, sir. If this happens each time I ride, I may need a new set of clothes every week." Remembering his kindness, she softened and took a deep breath. How could she stay angry while gazing into those eyes, so full of life but also so full of sadness? "Would you be kind enough to get down and help me, or must I sit here rubbing my ankle alone?"

His face darkened when his gaze strayed to her ankle. He immediately slipped off Storm and dropped on one knee. "You are hurt?" His face grimaced as he balanced on his bad leg. But before waiting for her answer, he lifted her easily into his arms and began an inspection of her foot.

"I am fine, other than my pride being a bit bruised. I merely twisted my ankle under me. The boot prevented further injury. But thank you." Her manner softened. "And thank you for the clothes. What a kind gift. I hope you'll accept my apology for being so curt." Once they were married, he might take her riding each day—at least, she hoped he would. She must be a mess. Running fingers through the hair on the sides of her head, she bit down on her lip. She was making it worse.

His hands gripped her arms as she stood to her feet. "Are you sure you can walk?"

"I've been worse. Though I could use help mounting Winter."

He eased her into the saddle, taking care to gently place her foot in the stirrup. His hand lingered on her ankle until their eyes met. Payton swallowed hard but didn't turn the horse away. She could feel warmth from his hand all the way through her boot. She was about to open her mouth when he spoke.

"We should get back. The men and I were in the middle of surveying the property to see if we could find any poachers. Or any...late-night screamers."

She kicked his hand away playfully. "And I was the best you came up with?"

His crooked smile, a result of the scar, teased back as he steadied Storm. "We found no one. No one but this strange boy suddenly flying across the meadow on Winter. If only he could tell us his story, maybe we would learn deep, dark secrets."

"His is not a story you would find interesting. But what of yours? Does it contain deep, dark secrets?"

A somber gloom overtook his face as he leaped into the saddle. "Not worth the telling."

In a pleasant change of pace, after a busy day of entertaining, the night held no more screams, no more meetings in the hallway, no more near kisses, no more surprises. Payton found she was content but also a bit disappointed. Sleep coming amid calm would be welcome. Tomorrow she'd wed. And she wanted to appear her best even though she realized it meant nothing at all to Jonathan. Did the marriage mean anything to her? Why should it? He was arrogant, overbearing and controlling. She gazed at the leather breeches on the back of the chair. And kind, caring, handsome and generous. She doubled a fist and punched the coverlet.

Her room comforted her with a lovely soothing quality. A soft bed and plump pillows. Fresh flowers each day, when available, and space to grow. She would miss it. Or would she be staying in this room indefinitely? Would he even be faithful? She hadn't thought about that. After all, he was doing all this just for her. So she would be safe. But he had emotions. Perhaps he would go on seeing Miss Anne. Oh, surely not.

Anne didn't love him. She had hovered over Payton all day, offering to help her. Likely that was all an act for Jonathan's benefit.

Well, she intended to be faithful. A marriage for whatever reason still included vows to God. She would mean them but what about Jonathan? They hadn't actually discussed the particulars. Here she was, marrying a man she had been afraid of her entire life, and she didn't know what their personal arrangements might be. She blushed. What *did* he expect from her?

She twisted her leg to find a restful position. Her ankle was tender, but it would not stop sleep from coming after such a long day. Blessed sleep to escape the concerns about tomorrow night.

Jonathan put his glass on the side table and offered the men cigars. He didn't care for them, but he always kept a box for visitors. He wished Wallace had not accompanied Anne. Was he jealous of Wallace Fitzhugh? Not at all. He was angry toward him. Now that he knew the ways of his late wife, he felt Wallace might have merely followed suit. He should dislike the man intensely, but he saw through Anne's game and decided not to snap at the bait. Had she honestly thought a marriage might have been in their future?

"Gentleman, I've a long day tomorrow. I believe I'll go to my room. A good night's sleep should provide welcome company. If you'll excuse me."

He leaped the stairs like a stag on mountain crags in

spite of the pain in his leg and stopped a moment outside Payton's door. Perhaps he should knock, but she must already be sleeping. As he stared at her closed door, he remembered holding her last night, protecting her, promising her a life of kindness. And before then? He had nearly kissed her. So close, her breath stirred against his mouth. He'd felt the warmth as she waited with her eyes closed for him to press his lips against hers.

He gripped his fist. Thinking about it only made matters worse. There would be no kisses, no hugs of encouragement and solace, no passion between them. Only long days and even longer nights when they lived as husband and wife in name only. He leaned against her door, bit down on his lip and cursed himself silently for the arrangement he had planned.

*God, if You are really there, can You forgive me? I never meant for this to come about in such a manner. I wanted to help and now, it seems, I have imprisoned us both. I shall not lie tomorrow but be truthful. When the time comes to test my fidelity, I don't want to hurt Payton. But a marriage to protect her will test me every day of my life.*

He bemoaned his circumstances. There was no God, so why did he waste his time praying? A loving God would have saved his marriage to Alithea, would have at least saved her life.

Now, he would never have a proper marriage. Never know a wife. Never share a moment when he might reach for her, laugh with her, love her. He knew his opportunities had come and gone, but Payton deserved better. Her being trapped in a loveless marriage caused him pain. But what other option was there? Her uncle, if indeed he were her uncle, had plans for her that would cause her to fare far worse. A groan burst through his lips with such intensity he spun about to be sure no one had heard.

There was nothing to be done but to think of her as his ward, as a child. In that way he wouldn't allow himself to be put in a situation like the other night, when he had kissed her. A child. The solution was right in front of him. She *was* a child. Wearing pants to ride, hair flying in the wind. He pictured her thusly so as not be tempted. Riding straddled in breeches with no care for propriety, she did resemble a very young girl. Pink cheeks, loud laughter, blue eyes, soft skin. Errgh. This would not be an easy task.

With steps heavier than Storm's, he stomped across the landing, stalked to his room and shouldered through the door, where he sat in the dark. He would beat this feeling. And when he did, he promised himself never to allow the raw emotions to rear up again.

## Chapter 8

Payton listened. Pans clanked in the kitchen below. The smells. The wonderful smells of a feast, and while she longed to be part of the gaiety the preparations produced, Emily had insisted she stay in her room so she and Jonathan would not cross paths. A long soak in a hot bath before Clarisse helped with her hair would pass the time. A quick look in the mirror decided the style for her. Pulling the fullness forward and covering the wild, short curls at the side should do. They might peek from under, but the thickness of her hair glowing with pride would tell on-lookers that Payton Whittard knew who she was.

She looked forward to wearing the lovely pearls Jonathan had bought, her arms filled with beautiful winter roses from the greenhouse. She'd have white roses for a bouquet and for her hair. She clapped her hands at the thought of the grand walk down the long staircase in such fine attire.

A small knock pulled her from her daydreams, and she caught herself smiling at the door. It must be Clarisse with the steaming water for her bath.

Mrs. Brewster's voice called from the hall. "Payton, dear. I have some tea with cream, fresh bread, shortbread cookies and butter sweetened with clover honey. Come to the door. Clarisse will be up with hot water and rose petals for your bath in about an hour. Eat, dear. Keep up your strength for the party tonight."

Payton hesitated. Keep her strength up? For tonight?

"Miss Payton. The door, please?"

She padded over the floor and invited Mrs. Brewster in for more than bread and tea. She needed to speak with a woman, and Anne wasn't even a consideration. "I hope you brought two cups."

Mrs. Brewster's face creased in a conspiratorial smile. "I planned ahead. Here, dearie. With plenty of honey and cream for you." She offered Payton the tea and retired to a chair by the fire with her own cup steaming in her hands.

"I'm sorry there's not much room. The copper tub is so big. I have never had a bath in such a tub before. You all will spoil me."

"You deserve spoiling, if you don't mind my saying so. And the master thinks so, too."

A sigh racked her body before she quelled the shudder. "I am not so sure. I'm never certain what he is thinking." Although he had bought her the dress and pearls and, best of all, the breeches and jacket, she was still troubled by what his true intentions might be.

Mrs. Brewster sipped her tea and nibbled one of the raspberry shortbread cookies; Payton withered under her gaze. "I can read your face, dearie. You of all folks know I speak the truth. He has made the entire manor available for you and your comfort. He is changing his entire life to offer you his full protection."

He had done that. True. But what she wanted she couldn't find in a box with ribbons. Her sense of being a woman had been awakened and she ached to be loved. The way her parents had loved each other every day through good and bad. Why couldn't she have that familiar comforting relationship? "May I ask you a question?"

"Of course."

She plucked a piece of the shortbread but finally left it on her plate. Dare she ask? "What caused Mrs. Lambrick's death?"

Mrs. Brewster's hand shook ever so slightly. "We shouldn't speak of such things. Should the master choose to tell you in time, he will."

So many secrets. Had he been involved in his wife's death? Oh, well, not today. No thinking on such things on her wedding day. She sighed. "I don't have a mother to prepare me. Will you come up to dress me after my bath? I should love your help."

Mrs. Brewster leaned forward, pressed a prim kiss on Payton's cheek and nodded. "I would love nothing more, dearie. Nothing more at all." She brushed at her own cookie crumbs along with some moisture in her eyes, set her cup on the tray and rose with effort from the chair. "Ring when you need me."

Jonathan brushed a missed spot of lint from the shoulder of his jacket. He stared at the craggy face in the mirror. Could she grow to love him in time? Despite the scar, he appeared acceptable. But nearly a decade separated them. Would that make a difference to her? Tonight, when he took his vows before his friends and God, he would mean them. And he would make every effort to offer her a life of happiness. Like a doting brother or favorite cousin. He would do his best to indulge her, laugh with her, pet her, but never truly love her, not as he would like. What he liked reached across miles of emotions and he couldn't allow himself even a taste of what pleased him. If he did, there would be no going back. The feelings would blossom once more and leave him as vulnerable as he had been to Alithea.

He tensed head to toe, slammed his fist on the dressing table. No. Not again. Not ever again.

When he entered the great hall, the sight stopped him. Evergreens filled each and every corner with tiny candles waiting to be lit. Red bows and berries dotted the greens. Silver vessels filled with white roses clustered on every table. He had told Mrs. Brewster to spare no expense or effort, and he was convinced the results would be pleasing to Payton.

He expected an array of friends from London as well as those from Colchester. Not since Alithea died had he assembled a ball such as this for Christmas. Their last Christmas together had been one of pure joy. So very much in love. No. He had been in love. What Alithea had felt, he was no longer sure. He sighed and turned toward the entrance.

Little by little guests arrived, their carriages following dozens of torches that lined the road for as far as he could see. Women in stunning gowns languished on the arms of their escorts. Jonathan envied the smiles and intimate exchanges that passed between some of them and wished for Payton to look at him the same.

At seven o'clock baskets and silver trays of food suddenly appeared on long tables against the wall. Hams dripped with maple glaze and turkeys with cranberry stuffing. Leg of lamb and cold venison perched under fruit towers with sugar sprinkled down the sides. Large platters held stuffed cakes and tarts to tempt the stodgiest of his guests. Punch filled cut-glass bowls and crystal ladles and cups waited on smaller tables at each end of the hall. Jonathan smiled his approval at the job Mrs. Brewster had done in such a short time. And Clarisse. Her work often went unrewarded but not tonight. On Christmas they both would receive a very tangible show of his appreciation.

As he left for the hall to greet a new round of guests, he stopped. And wondered. Payton, still absent, worried him. Would the boyish, childish version of Payton show up, or might the gown be filled with a beautiful young woman anxious to be married? Before he finished speculating, she appeared at the top of the steps. The guests filing through the entrance stopped in the hallway at the bottom of the staircase and gasped collectively as their lines of vision drew immediately to the beautiful woman at the pinnacle of the room.

She hesitated on the landing, smiled in Jonathan's direction with a blush across her cheeks and started her descent. The gown swayed when she walked, and he could make out the tops of the kid slippers. Her pearls contrasted with the blue in the gown so they shone in the candlelight like dozens of exquisite jewels. Her eyes sparkled as the brightest blue he had ever seen. When she arrived at the bottom, he swallowed hard and offered his arm. Leaning to her ear, his lips brushed her skin, making his stomach clench when he whispered, "You take my breath away, Payton. You are so beautiful."

She glanced up, rather shyly, with a welcome he hadn't expected. "Thank you, Jonathan." Then she leaned closer and whispered for only him to hear, "Sir Jonathan."

His heart hammered in his chest, and he tried to calm

the heavy beating. This wasn't in his plan. Taking deep breaths, he did his utmost to think about her in breeches instead of the gown. Anything to keep his mind from where it longed to go. The strategy wasn't working; the way she looked, the smell of roses on her skin, her hair curling around her face and falling heavily against the gown... His thoughts rammed a steady rhythm inside and if he didn't stop, he would give away all those feelings for the world to see.

He turned quickly away from her and faced their guests. "Mr. and Mrs. Hathaway, I'd like to introduce Miss Payton Whittard. Payton, these are friends from Colchester. They knew your father, I believe." There now, a chance to stop and calm his heart.

Mrs. Hathaway spoke for both of them. "Yes. Why, we have one of your father's bitches. The best in all of Essex County. It is very nice to meet you, my dear. I understand you helped your father raise them. I have always felt he who can love an animal with a gentle hand is a fine human being."

Payton's blush did her honor. "You are kind to speak so of my father. He is missed as are his animals. I have only the puppy Hope left. And Hunter. They will be the start of a new generation. A herald of the new life to come." Her wan smile tore Jonathan's heart in two.

He had not thought enough of the cost to Payton. Of course she had a heart of gold. And she had lost so much without ever complaining. Here she stood, obviously frightened out of her wits to be marrying a man she barely knew, and she was talking of new life. Of course, she would want children one day. How callous of him not to be thinking of her feelings instead of his own. And with their arrangement, there would, of course, be no children.

* * *

Once she had received all of their guests, Payton wandered into the great hall; her breath caught in her throat. Candles dotted the room like tiny jewels, and ribbons and greens adorned the doorways and tables in such a lovely way she might have fainted had she not held on tightly to Jonathan's arm. So attentive. Almost embarrassingly so, but isn't that what he had said he planned to do? Out to fool the rest of the world. As long as he didn't try to fool her into thinking this marriage was more than it was.

The musicians began playing and she easily joined in the dancing, though she had never learned to do it well. Jonathan leaned toward her when she winced at a mistake. "If you had your breeches on, you would glide across the floor with no problems."

She raised her brow and shrugged a shoulder; he was right. Anne floated with her partner and Payton longed to be able to do the same. Dresses and skirts simply got in the way. "I do wish I had this gown off."

He leaned in and smiled.

She felt her eyes widen and she blushed. She almost missed the amusement on his face when Anne drew near. Of course, he was just playing the game.

"Jonathan, darling. We haven't had one dance together. Would you be kind enough, Payton, to allow a favorite sister to dance with her brother-in-law?"

Payton loosened her grip and he drifted onto the floor with Anne. Round and round they danced, synchronized perfectly as if they had danced every day of their lives, though Payton saw how he struggled to move smoothly. He must be hurting. Once they finished, Caroline grasped his arm and soon he dashed from one young lady to another, dance after dance, swirl after swirl, ever the devoted host, leaving Payton to sit and visit with her guests. Well, if he was in pain, he deserved it.

Mrs. Merriwether laughed to see him twirling through steps with her granddaughter. Her hands plopped into her lap with finality. "I often thought he would make a good husband for Julia," she said with a shake of her head. "But you have captured his heart, it seems. You are a lovely addition to Kent Hall, my dear."

Did it appear to Mrs. Merriwether she had captured his heart? Surely not. Payton felt just the opposite. Once again, he seemed more to be the eligible bachelor than a doting fiancé. She was being a foolish girl and knew it, but while her head accepted their arrangement, her heart continued to fight it.

"Thank you, Mrs. Merriwether." She glanced toward the dance floor. Jonathan had disappeared once again. With which lady this time?

"Did you have a nice visit?" His voice floated low and velvety smooth behind her. He no doubt spoke that way to all his partners. Still, her heart responded in spite of her efforts to quell the beating as his hand cupped her elbow.

"I had nothing else to do for the past two hours. So, yes, I had a lovely visit."

"Ah, Payton, child. You still don't trust me, do you? And I seem to have forgotten myself once again. I shall not leave your side for the remainder of the evening. Will that please you, or do I have to beg your attention?"

Without wanting to, her eyes snapped like sparks in a fire. Two could play at this game. And she would show him just how adept she could be for a *child*. She looked up and reached for Mr. Fitzhugh's arm as he passed by. "Mr. Fitzhugh, I believe you're ignoring me. I have need of a tutor on the dance floor. And I have heard you are quite the dance partner. Would you mind showing me how this reel is done?"

His eyes darted from Payton to Jonathan and then back to Payton again. His tongue tickled his upper lip with a smile and he bowed low. "I would be honored, dear lady."

Jonathan's gaze never left the dance floor. He kept her in his vision as she skipped her slippers to the rhythm of the music with one partner after another. He grasped the intent of her actions but felt helpless against the emotions they evoked. He could almost hear her telling him *two could play at this game.* He had been available to many women these past five years, doing his best to forget Alithea, but there was something in Payton the others had lacked. Integrity? Honesty? All that and more. Without trying—in fact, trying not to—he was falling in love with this beautiful creature who had landed defenselessly on his doorstep.

He ran his tongue over dry lips. What she was doing to him. He wouldn't give in to the struggle any longer. Tonight, when they were alone, he would admit to her how he felt, and he prayed she would admit the same. For now, they would continue their charade.

"Jonathan, it's almost midnight. Is the vicar here yet?" Anne fluffed the sleeves of her gown and gazed into his eyes.

"He's waiting in the library. If I don't trim the wings on my little falcon, she may want to keep floating over the dance floor." But he had deserved her censure after having, once again, left her to herself when he should have gathered her in his arms and glided over the floor with her, showing her how much he cared.

Anne nudged him. "Jonathan? Her flowers have been

placed on the chair in the corner. Is there anything else I can do?"

"You have been a great help already. I hardly know how to thank you."

She stood on her toes and before he could stop her, she pulled his head down and kissed him on the mouth. "That is a good start. You won't forget me after tonight, I hope."

Jonathan's breath hitched. "Anne! I'm being married tonight." One minute a friend, the next vexing him. Surely she jested.

"I cannot see what that has to do with anything, darling."

Thank goodness Payton had joined Mrs. Brewster in the library to speak with the vicar. She would have had plenty to say about that kiss. And rightfully so.

A light tap on his shoulder sent chills up his spine. It couldn't be. He watched the edges of Anne's face break into a knowing smile.

"I see you continue to be an attentive and gracious host, Jonathan."

He whipped about to face Payton, Mrs. Brewster and the vicar. "I try." Instead of being angry with himself, he was angry with the entire situation. He wanted to kiss someone all right, and it wasn't Anne Newbury. That could never happen again. Instead of defending his behavior as he should have, he stood his ground offensively.

Payton's lip curled just enough for him to notice. Leaning down, he murmured in her ear, "So you want me attentive? Always be careful for what you wish." Sweat tickled his forehead and he did his best not to let her see what he was really thinking. If she could, she would control the rest of his life, and no woman must be allowed to do that again. No. No late-night conversation about his love for her. He had to keep her at bay.

His arm signaled the musicians and his eyes swept the room. "Ladies and gentlemen, you were invited here tonight for two reasons. For a Christmas ball, to be sure, to celebrate in the traditional Lambrick style, but also to join us for the wedding of Jonathan Michael Lambrick and Payton Elizabeth Whittard."

Air whistled through surprised mouths, along with gasps and ahhs. Jonathan held up one hand and smiled. "She is a most beautiful partner, is she not? If you would be kind enough to let the vicar through, we shall take our vows." He tugged her hand into his and walked toward the end of the great hall, where a canopy of flowers had been placed for the occasion.

The applause followed thunderously, but he had to practically drag Payton along. His grip tightened and he spoke through gritted teeth. "Payton, this is not the time to make a spectacle. Let us do this. Come with me."

Her eyes flashed, and he had not the slightest idea what she might say when the time came. Although, if he had come to know her at all, he had a few clues. Not waiting to find out, he soldiered her along.

Mrs. Brewster stepped forward and nestled the veil into Payton's hair with her mother's silver comb. Jonathan swallowed hard at the vision in his hands.

When he was asked if he took her for his bride, he made sure his "I do" was heard all the way to the back of the room. And he meant it. He pledged himself to her by the grace of God and his sincerity alone. She, however, murmured the words softly. But after the vicar finished the ceremony, Jonathan turned her to their guests, dipped his head and pulled her so close the breath whooshed from her chest.

He might only have one chance, so it would have to last a while. She drew back, but his hands encircled her with pressure enough to snare the most unwelcome interest. She wanted attention; well, he would oblige. His lips brushed hers momentarily, forcing her to partake, and then the softness turned to urgency. He forgot where he was and pressed his mouth over hers, taking the only kiss he ever expected to willingly get. Her breath flowed into his until he couldn't tell where his started and hers stopped. There was faint applause and then a rumbling, but he barely heard it. His mouth continued to search for one sign of welcome, all the while crushing her lips with his. She started to struggle, but he kept her in his embrace.

At last, the vicar cleared his throat and laughed with a nervous half word of congratulations until laughter overwhelmed the room. Jonathan drew himself up, glanced about and stared into Payton's eyes. Hurt and shame reflected back to him. He offered his arm once more, leaned over and said in a voice only she could hear, "Always take care what you wish." He had made a spectacle of both of them, and he wished he could take the kiss back, but, of course, that was impossible.

Once again he had caused her grief, when all he longed for was to keep her in his arms, the rest of the world leaving them alone. This was his wife, his love. But telling her would be his undoing. No, she could never know how he felt. One kiss and that was all.

# *Chapter 9*

Payton received good wishes from her departing guests. When the last well-wisher climbed into a carriage, she closed the door and lifted her chin. Her hands tightened at her sides. If he wanted a battle, she must supply one. Embarrassing her in such a way. She wasted no time but ran directly to the staircase and flew up the steps as if wings lifted her slippers.

She stopped a moment to stare at the gold band on her finger. She would gladly pitch it in his face, but no, that would never do. There remained houseguests who still believed them to be happily married. Fully and wholly married if that kiss were any indication.

When she lingered outside the door to her room, she listened. He was supposed to be staying in the sitting room tonight so their friends would think they were sharing sleeping quarters. He must still be seeing to the cleanup of the hall. She entered, locked her door, slipped into the sitting room and unlocked that door, then returned to her own chamber. The dress fell from her shoulders and she donned a nightgown Mrs. Brewster had left on the bed. She sat in front of the mirror and removed pins from her hair. The full length of it fell onto her arms, the small side curls hidden by the chestnut mass. She hadn't noticed before how dark her hair was in the winter, but in the candlelight, it shone almost black.

A small rap at the door sent tingles down her back. "Go away. The sitting room's been prepared. Go away, Jonathan."

His steps didn't have a particularly happy ring to them. She held her breath. Soon, there came a rap at the closet. "Go away."

"Payton, open the door. Now!"

He had agreed to a marriage of convenience, so why was he pursuing her? She stepped to the door timidly and opened it but a crack. His haughty demeanor pushed away any apprehension she might have felt.

"May I come in?"

Her heart thudded, but she pulled the door open wide. "This is your house, Mr. Lambrick. I don't pretend to be able to keep you out." She turned and touched her lips with her fingers. If he would kiss her again, the arrangement might change. He had touched her heart so often lately, she imagined a full life with him, but she must never be a beggar and his womanizing ways would no doubt not end merely because of marriage vows.

"Payton, I only wanted to apologize. I seem to be doing that a lot lately. I should not have embarrassed you in front of my friends. Our friends. You were so beautiful, I am afraid I was carried away. I never meant to kiss you in such a manner." But his gaze said quite the opposite.

Her face flamed with indignation in spite of the

strange emotions tingling through her. So, he didn't really want to kiss her, he just got carried away? Payton moved slowly to the corner table where a vase of the white roses had been set. She fingered the petals and leaned to smell one of them. "You know, we have a way of taking care of animals who become too…enamored. Do you understand?"

"No."

"Then let me educate you." With her back turned, she yanked the roses from the vase and spun around, flipping water from his head to his toes. "A little cold water works miracles on an ardent hound." She retreated to the other side of the room and crossed her arms over her chest. She hoped the determination she felt showed on her face. Her mouth was set, ready for a fight.

Without a word, he grabbed the towel from the water pitcher, wiped his face and hands and dropped the towel on the floor. His look grew dark and sinister before her eyes. "If I may educate you now, Payton. Cold water has little effect on a man."

He strode across the floor in two long strides, his steps making clear he hadn't found her lesson very charming. "I have done all I know to please you. I have left you alone. I have stayed by your side. I have complimented you and ignored you. I don't know what you want, but I do know what I want. I promised before God and our guests tonight that I would be faithful, but I also promised to love only you."

His mouth crushed hers, searching for a response. He kissed her eyes, her forehead, her cheeks and then her lips again and again until she couldn't breathe. "I love you more than I have ever loved anyone. Payton, I do not want to live my life without you. I love you." He kissed her chin. "Love you." He kissed the tip of her nose. "Love you." Then his mouth settled gently on hers, like butter-fly wings softly overshadowing a flower.

She stumbled back, drawing in air, and pulled her hands to her mouth. Her lips still tingled and she wasn't sure what to say to wipe away the longing in his eyes. "We…had an agreement, sir." Her breath was coming in ragged gasps, and her heart felt as if it might explode in her chest. If only he meant it. What a life they might have.

He stared, eyes now full of…what? She wasn't sure. He repeated, "Jonathan. Not sir."

"We had an agreement, Jonathan. We would live together as friends."

"Then that is what you want?" His eyes snapped with fire that threatened.

She had a choice. Would he want what she longed for or was he playing one of his games? "I had thought—"

Suddenly it sounded as though screams poured from every corner of the house. Jonathan turned and ran into the hall. Payton stopped to put on a robe, then followed.

Further down the hallway, Anne stood amid a gaggle of the remaining guests in various states of dress, tears pouring over her cheeks. A thin pink wrapper exposed more than any woman should reveal to strangers. Jonathan removed the coat from his shoulders, damp though it was, and draped it around her.

"Oh, Jonathan. It was I who screamed. I saw a figure outside the window. A woman. She looked like…like Alithea." She clutched at him and buried her face in his chest. When he attempted to break free, her tears started in earnest and she gripped him with more intensity until her arms completely encircled him.

"Nonsense, Anne. You're being foolish. Someone is taking great strides to destroy my life and perhaps even

Kent Park. I still think Payton's uncle is involved in this. You men—" he pointed at the London party "—come with me. We will all begin a search in earnest."

Small steps padded quietly along the hallway, and he strained to see past Anne's head. The hurt look on Payton's face when she recognized Anne in his arms left him trembling. "Payton!"

She jutted her chin out, turned on her heel and rushed back to her room, where she closed the door with less than a delicate hand.

Having nearly succumbed to his advances, Payton stomped her foot and hit the door with her palm. For a few minutes, she had believed they might have a true and meaningful marriage, but ten minutes later, she discovered Anne, once again, in his arms. Payton didn't consider herself a fool; not for one second did she doubt Anne instigated these moments to upset her, but Jonathan wasn't a naive young boy, either. He had to acknowledge Anne's maneuverings. Did Anne remind him so much of Alithea that he couldn't resist? Or was there more to their history?

Jonathan seemed a godly man. Was he?

She pouted as she made her way to the window. There she pulled back heavy velvet drapes and stared into the darkness. Figures on horseback roamed the night, and she spotted Jonathan at once. He had obviously formed a party of the men tonight instead of in the morning.

A light rap at her door startled her. "Payton, it's Anne. Are you awake?"

Should she answer? Well, why not? After all, she was Jonathan's wife now. "A moment, please."

As they met in the open doorway, Payton stepped aside. Anne moved hesitantly through the door, where she crossed the floor to take the seat nearest the fire. She looked at the neatly made bed. "I've come to apologize."

Payton's brow shot up. "Anne, I am generally not an unkind person, but without Jonathan here, why don't you speak in earnest?"

"Please sit down. I have a long story to tell and I would hope at the end of it, you might judge whether or not to trust me."

Payton settled into the wingback chair and allowed the fire to reach out and warm her face. Or was it anger that brought heat to her cheeks?

"Five years ago, Jonathan and Alithea engaged in an argument not missed by any in attendance. His anger licked through Kent that night like a roaring blaze, and she dashed to the stables for safety. Once there, Birdie readied a carriage. She fled in the darkness and over-turned at Bay Lane, the same place your parents lost their lives. I do not believe she would have lost control of the buggy had Jonathan not been chasing her on horse-back, trying to force her return. I will give him his due, he tried to save her and ended up disfigured for it, but she should never have been in that carriage running for her life if not for him."

Payton stared at the fire, her thoughts a jumble. "I didn't realize. I did hear things…when his wife died."

"I thought perhaps I could make his life a bit miser-able and spoil his intentions with you…for your sake, of course. I do not want to see you in the bottom of the gully, where I am convinced Alithea's spirit still walks the glen."

"Surely you don't believe such nonsense."

"Perhaps not."

Payton hadn't witnessed a malicious side of Jonathan. Oh, she had feared him before she knew him, but he had never been cruel, only stern and unyielding. And she supposed strong principles must be behind the uncompromising demeanor. Yet, Anne had enjoyed personal moments with him, enough to know his inner self. "There must be a logical reason for the disturbances. But I appreciate you coming here and explaining how your sister died. He hasn't shared with me any details."

"You have a right to know. And Payton?"

"Yes?"

"You can be sure he did not only marry you as a favor to your father."

The woman spoke in riddles. Jonathan had no special bond with her father other than that her father raised hounds for him. "What favor to my father?"

"Why, just before your father died on the road, he insisted Jonathan promise to do whatever he could to protect you. Didn't he tell you?"

Payton heard the door to the sitting room open and close softly. Heard Jonathan remove his boots with a groan. Heard the sound of water splash into the bowl. Heard him sigh when he stretched upon the settee. His leg and shoulder must still hurt very much.

She could picture him struggling to fit his well-muscled body onto the dainty chaise. If she opened the door and invited him into her chamber, what would he do? He might not even acknowledge her, and if Anne were correct, he was more than capable of overpowering her in a way that could destroy her life—or what was left of it. She could always change places with him; she would fit tolerably on the chaise with room to spare. If only he had been honest with her about her father, she might invite him in once and for all, but the newfound knowledge of his lying roused a nasty attitude in her. One she would have to pray about to dispel.

She crept close to the door adjoining the rooms. "Jonathan? Are you awake still?"

"Yes."

"May I come in?" She entered and immediately recognized a darkness settling in his eyes. He rose and crossed the small space. "You would be more comfortable in the bed."

He hesitated and his lip curled at the edges, accentuating the scar. "I have no doubt."

As she moved across the room, he reached out, but she continued past him to the chaise and settled onto it.

"But I thought—"

Payton, most of the time generous to a fault, would not makes excuses for lies. Her mother had taught her forgiveness for almost anything, but not lying. Why hadn't he told her about his promise to her father? "Good night, Jonathan."

What a plan. How had he believed this could ever work? She was stubborn, opinionated, far too emotional to be sensible, naive, pigheaded, childish and downright insufferable! And he had taken her as his wife. The uncle? Had the uncle been real, or was he someone Payton had hired to finagle her way into Kent Hall permanently? No, he knew enough of her to understand that wasn't true, but why, then, was she driving him mad, little by little, day by day? Kiss by kiss. He punched the pillow and slammed his head against it.

The outlandish kiss in front of the assemblage…if only he had not kissed her. A brotherly peck would have been more than sufficient. Until that moment, he had been able to control his feelings. But his pride and indignation singled out her behavior with Wallace, behavior that mimicked Alithea's with Patrick Dowdy the night she died. Kissing another man!

Five years ago he had walked in to discover Alithea entangled with Dowdy just as she had been with Wallace before their wedding. The man had been kissing her, fondling her. He had chased her to the stable, mounted Ebony, who was the mount closest to him, and rode after her carriage. Dowdy had whipped the horses as they fled. As Jonathan rounded the bend at Bay Lane, he heard her screaming at Dowdy when the carriage rolled over and over. Down the gully they'd floundered.

When he fought Patrick Dowdy, the man had pulled a dagger, stabbed him repeatedly in the arms as he tried to protect himself and then slashed Jonathan's face. With one stinging blow, Jonathan had smashed the side of the man's head, stopping any further attack, but the damage had been done. Dowdy snatched Ebony's reins and galloped away, leaving Alithea and Jonathan bathed in blood and lies. Jonathan hadn't the heart to ruin his dead wife's reputation by reporting the truth. He hid the wounds on his arms and blamed the axle of the carriage for the gash on his face.

Was Payton merely another Alithea—a woman who would stop at nothing to get what she wanted? If so, what did she want? She had been adamant at the beginning she wanted no part of living at Kent Hall. He shook his head. He would not believe the worst. After all, this entire charade had been his doing. One day, if he worked hard enough, she might view him as a man disposed to love her, anxious to love her, longing to love her. In the meantime, he would respect her privacy. Another bed would be moved into his quarters. No one would be the wiser but Mr. Kenny and Mrs. Brewster. He would have long drapes hung in front of her bed. She would have her own area, and he could sleep at night close enough to protect her but without having to watch the face of an angel.

Sleeping on the chaise each night would soon have her aching in places she did not even appreciate existed. She would speak to him in the morning about a better way to continue their pretense. Once she reached her twenty-first birthday, she would answer to no one. She was loath to do so now.

Hitting the back of the chaise—hard—she twisted around until it was nearly bearable. She moaned softly. At long last, on her wedding night, she drifted off to sleep—alone.

## Chapter 10

Payton slid quietly into her chamber. Empty. Jonathan must have awakened early and was now gone. For the past four days he had been up early and out on his land. Avoiding her? Surprised by her disappointment, she slid into her chair, slipped soft slippers onto her feet and glanced in the mirror. Was she sufficiently attractive for her handsome husband?

Her husband—the word made the hairs on her arms tickle her skin in a pleasant way. Would he stay married to her after her uncle was no longer a threat? A few more minutes and she would play new bride again, smiling and flattering the last of their guests, praying Jonathan would join, not only in the charade, but in what life had to offer them.

On the stand by the window where she had discarded them, her bouquet of white roses lay crumpled and nearing death. Fingering the petals, she recognized their love would die, too, without nourishment. It might never have life in the first place. And after what Anne had told her, she was more confused than ever. She lifted the silver comb he had brought back from her parents' cottage and skimmed her fingers over the cool smoothness. Her hand shook. She pulled the comb through her hair and shivered as she recalled the night of the ball. She was married, whether or not she liked it, whether or not love ever became part of it. And, in truth, she didn't know how that made her feel. When she closed her eyes, his lips were still warm on hers. But how could that be? He had not meant the kiss, had not meant the tenderness. He had kissed her to show her who was in control.

She glanced again at her image and despised the frown staring back. The kiss had embarrassed her, had embarrassed their guests and should have embarrassed Jonathan. Now, his indifference wriggled under her skin. Before she could control her temper, she threw the comb so hard, she cracked the edge of the mirror.

Storm thundered across the meadow, his mane flying against Jonathan's hands. Jonathan stopped abruptly and slid from the saddle. The sun pushed the cold away and, for a moment, he thrived under the warmth of the rays. More warmth than the marriage offered. He knelt to pick a dead flower from the ground. Dead, like his hopes. Only the kiss remained, a reminder of what he was missing. Of the love he was sure he'd felt breathed from her lips to his. But she had shut out any opportunity he'd had to comfort her and apologize for humiliating her. That's all he wanted to do. He would have held her until she slept, but no, she'd have no part of him. Were all women so fickle they couldn't decide what they wanted? Well, until she knew, they would live under pretense.

The five days since their wedding he had slept in her room and she in the sitting room. If only Payton would come to him. He would pet her, shower her with gifts, give her anything she wanted.

Before he left for the day, he ordered a bed be moved to his room. Mr. Kenny brought Birdie from the stable and assisted Mrs. Brewster in the details before their guests arose. If Payton wanted brother and sister, she would get it. But how long would that be sufficient for a young woman? Would she not desire children, a real and true family? And if she did, that would mean her leaving him, like everyone else in his life. Well, he'd have none of that.

His arms stretched above his head as he scrutinized the land. His land. He owed it to his tenants to give his full attention to the day-to-day workings so they could all live good lives. His preoccupation with Payton had kept him from his duties. No more.

He mounted Storm and headed for the glen. He would ride all day if necessary to clear her from his head and to avoid facing Payton and his guests and start the falsehood again. He was not anxious to return to the manor.

Payton remained out of doors as her last guest entered his carriage and rode away. Anne had been the first to leave the day after the ball, which surprised Payton. Anne never seemed far away from Jonathan.

And now he was absent. Perhaps business had distracted him from his household duties.

She retreated to the house, where she quickly donned her breeches and the black boots, which supported her tender ankle well. She brushed at a smudge on the leather and sighed deeply. A spot. A blemish. Just like her. A blemish on his life. A fool's errand he had become embroiled in from a sense of honor to her father and nothing more. She stomped her foot and cried; the ankle was still tender. She drew on gloves and slipped into her jacket. Allowing her hair to fly loose, she liked the way it covered the sides of her head. Only small curls peeked out as reminders of the fire.

After grabbing a buttered wedge of pumpernickel bread from the kitchen, she dashed for the stable and soon stood opposite Birdie with Winter ready for a long ride. She would put Jonathan, their guests and even Kent out of her mind for a few hours. Birdie helped her up, and she immediately pulled the bit to turn Winter out of the stable. The horse's muscles moved them hastily away from the one place that tortured her mind while drawing her back again and again.

Winter galloped and spit up dirt with her hooves, but Payton had no intention of reining her in. The wind blew her hair, kissed her lips with the pure freshness of the morning and lulled her toward the glen, where she could sit in what was left of the soft grass while Winter ate her fill. Though the nights were cold, the days of late had an almost balmy warmth of which she couldn't wait to feel on her face.

Jonathan stretched again, tired from the sleepless night, as the sun tickled his face and encouraged him to loll on the crisp grass and forget how strangely his life had changed. A month ago he had been in charge, loved no one, answered to no one, and now, now he was a husband. Or a protector? A brother? He wasn't quite sure which.

Storm lifted his head and Jonathan did the same. A rider. Perhaps one of his guests come to drag him back.

He eased behind the skeletal network of wild raspberry bushes.

The rider drew closer but settled far away from Jonathan, obviously unable to see him. But he saw her. Payton. When Winter shook her head, sending her mane flying in the air, Payton did the same, and he smiled at her wild abandon. She dropped easily from the saddle, tethered Winter and dropped onto the bank of the brook, where the grass was mostly short and dry. And she, like a foal, rolled on the ground with sheer joy. From what he knew of her, she was no doubt thrilled to be out of a confining gown.

He laughed. If she could see herself. If she knew he was watching, she would probably scratch his eyes out, but he couldn't bring himself to look away. At times, she behaved like such a child, like a favorite little sister, but at others, she proved herself to be a remarkable woman, a beautiful woman full of life and wonder. Before long, she slept peacefully.

With as much stealth as he could muster, he rose and walked quietly to her side. Still she slept. At last, he stooped next to her and brushed the hair from her eyes. She started and blinked. Then she drew up on an elbow, eyes wide with surprise. "Jonathan?"

He frowned. She was upset to see him. "Yes, Jonathan. Your husband, Payton."

Pulling up fully to a sitting position and hugging her arms around her knees, she glanced away, her eyes drawn to Winter. "I am aware you're my husband, Jonathan." Her bottom lip trembled, and he longed to soothe her, tell her everything would be all right, but he wasn't sure she would appreciate his efforts. Nor was he sure it was true.

He picked a strand of ryegrass and nibbled the tip; it was too dry, but he continued to hold it in his mouth. It helped to keep him from grabbing her and kissing her as he would have liked. Every fiber of his being longed to hold her. "You're out early. Have the last of our guests gone home?"

"Without your help, yes, they have."

"I didn't think you wanted me there playing house with you." He cleared his throat. He had to stop goading her into an argument each time they met.

She looked away. "I didn't expect you to *play house* with me, Jonathan. I simply thought you would want to be hospitable. Not to worry—I told them you had work to attend on the property."

"Oh." She could have made him look bad to their guests, but she had chosen to offer a polite explanation to release him from his duties. That hurt more than a slap.

At last, he moved so that he knelt in front of her and she didn't turn away. He reached cautiously for her hands, lifted them to his face and touched them ever so gently with his lips. She shuddered and glanced down.

"Payton, I am a man of limited experience with love. I have no idea how to tell you what is in my heart."

Her eyes welled. He had made a mess of things once again. "Please don't cry. I don't ever want to see you cry." Winter nickered and huffed as if calling him a liar.

"Jonathan, when I rode out here, it was to decide whether or not to run away. Sharing quarters in Kent Hall with you is impossible. I cannot sleep in your room and be your sister. When I took our vows, I—"

"Shh." He pulled her into his arms. "You needn't say another word."

"But I do. It is just so difficult to tell you. I don't understand what I'm feeling."

He held her head against his chest and felt the trembling that coursed through both of them. His hands played in her hair, calming and quieting her the best way he knew. "Payton, you are heart of my heart, breath of my breath. Not a friend, a ward or a sister. None of that for us, Payton. I love you as though you had been a part of me before we were born."

She leaned back to see his face. "Do you mean that?"

"Yes, I do." He freed his arms and softly, so as not to frighten her, cupped her face in his hands. She was so small, so tender. His heart felt as if it were being crushed in his chest. "You are more important to me than my own life."

"And I love you, Sir Jonathan."

He laughed as his arms encircled her again before she could say another word. She leaned against him. His lips sought hers, gently, reverently endeavoring to convince her of his love. He held her so near, felt the beating of their hearts melt together like gentle wings strumming the air in rhythm.

She returned the embrace and sighed against his shoulder.

His eyes squeezed shut. "How could you love me?" When he opened them, he groaned. "Look at me."

Her head lifted, and she stared with a smile that could have imprisoned him if only she knew her power over him. "I'm looking."

"Women love me for my money, not my appearance."

She ran a finger over his eye, his cheek and his lip where the scar could not be hidden. "Then you have known foolish women in your past. I love you with all of your imperfections as I hope you love me." She kissed the edge of his lip where the scar ended. "You are the handsomest man I have *ever* known, not that it would matter about how I feel." She thought he was handsome.

Digging into the innermost depth of his chest, he

sighed aloud. "Imperfections? You have none." Her free spirit could never be mistaken for an imperfection, but he felt the less said the better at the moment.

"I have many as you are well aware. But if you will love me anyway, I will gladly be your wife in every sense of the word." Her finger hesitated before running along the scar from his cheek and his lips, where she once again kissed him.

Pulling off his greatcoat as he stood, he laid it on the grass. Then he gently slid her against it and cradled her in his arms.

He could no longer stop the emotions he had been restraining the past week. His lips pressed into hers and he realized how much sweeter she was than clover. She was an innocent and inviting contrast to his great strength, and he sought her full permission as his mouth pleaded with hers. And Jonathan understood the wedding vows for the first time in his life. Caring what they meant before God as he hadn't meant them when he married Alithea. Payton was his and he was hers. Hurting her would have meant destroying a piece of himself.

As his feelings fanned with expectation, he heard cries. "Sir. Come quickly!"

Jonathan pulled away from Payton, feeling his brow furrow in anger. Who would disturb them at such a time?

Birdie should not have interrupted them. Not even on Mrs. Brewster's orders.

Alithea's gown. How had it come to be in his room? Jonathan now had no doubt in his mind that someone wanted to destroy not only his relationship with Payton, but also Kent Hall. Who would plant this gown in his room?

Obviously, Mrs. Brewster had been frightened. Jonathan gave strict instructions for her to burn the gown before Payton saw it. Then he wasted no time in putting his chamber to rights in the hope that he and Payton might finally share their lives.

He barked orders at the downstairs maids, the upstairs maids and anyone else within the sound of his voice. Birdie and Mr. Kenny rushed once again to remove the extra furniture from his room. He instructed Mrs. Brewster that Payton's personal items should quickly find a home with his.

And certainly not Alithea's clothing. How had that happened?

Who was it planting items, filling his home with screams, scaring Payton? If he didn't discover the culprit soon, they had no chance of a calm life together. Not that it ever would be calm with a woman like Payton. He laughed to think of her flying across the meadows in men's breeches.

Once Birdie scurried away, Jonathan called Payton's name, not wanting her so much as a footstep from him.

When she arrived by his side, he scooped her into his arms. "Tell me, Payton. Say the words."

"What words?" She reached her arms out.

"Please tell me that you love me, dear one. I need to hear you say it."

She drew his head down and looking about her with a face flamed in red, she whispered in his ear, "I love you, dearest Jonathan." She touched his cheek with her fingertips and traced them along his face and across his lips. Her fingers lingered on his lip and she circled his mouth tenderly. "I shall love you forever."

As his arms tightened around her, he dipped his head closer to hers. "Was there ever a man so blessed as I? Was there ever a love so sweet, so complete as my love for you? Why has God seen fit to bring you to me, sweet and kind, loving and good? I don't deserve to be entrusted with your love."

"Oh, Jonathan. We are the only persons alive on this earth. The only two who ever knew love before. I swear, Jonathan. The only two."

His heart swelled, and he closed his eyes, her face overwhelming him with radiance. When he opened them again he said, "I want to be a better man for all my life. Anything for you."

"You would grant me anything I wished?"

If he could give her the Seven Wonders of the World he would, gladly. But he had only himself and Kent Park, poor substitutes. "Whatever is within my power."

"I would wish that we could stay here forever with our children and our grandchildren and even our great-grandchildren." Her blush reminded him that they must be truly alone before they could consider children and grandchildren. Sooner or later they must address the fact they were man and wife without servants and guests claiming his time.

"For now and for always, whatever you desire." He set her on the floor and held her at arm's length. His eyes took in the pink covering her cheeks. "But dearest one, we cannot live on love alone. We would become frail skeletons."

"Oh, Jonathan."

His stomach rumbled and he grinned. "Do you smell the venison roasting? I must admit, we have to go down for dinner or there will be talk. I am famished of a sudden."

"If you are to be properly cared for, allow me to go find Mrs. Brewster."

He smiled. After all, she was to be mistress of the house as well as the mistress of his heart.

Jonathan stood and pulled back her chair, not at the end of the table, but next to his. Payton's heart filled with pride at the attention he gave so freely, not as a ploy to fool outsiders. He offered her the plate of food Mrs. Brewster had prepared.

"Thank you, Jonathan." That he would wait on her and care enough to see to her needs surprised her. This giant of a man, caring about the little things.

She accepted the plate, and smelling the delicious odors of herb-crusted meat and vegetables, she realized how hungry the promise of the day had left her.

His eyes were on her as she inspected the food, but they sparked with mischief when he spoke. "Eat. Keep up your strength, Payton Lambrick. I intend to escort you shopping today." He leaned in and murmured in her ear. "New breeches. You must have another pair. And I have a present I must pick up."

She scowled but barely hid the grin at his affability. It would be difficult to hide her feelings from him. "A present? You are all kindness, sir. Will I forever be allowed the freedom of breeches when I ride about Kent?"

"As long as I am master of the house, you will be allowed whatever freedoms you wish. You are an intelligent woman, full of life, and I should never try to subdue you or ask you to compromise who you are. Together, we are one, neither more important than the other."

She wanted to believe him. But could she believe everything he said? Should she ask about the promise to her father? That niggling doubt continued to plague her. "Jonathan? Do you truly love me?"

He lounged forward in his chair and gazed into her

eyes. She quivered under his scrutiny. With his head resting in his hand, he smiled beneath his fingers. "I should
love you no matter what you took it into your beautiful
head to do. You are my other half, Payton. My better half
and nothing you do or say will ever change that. Certainly
not a pair of leather breeches. Is that what was bothering
you?" Sitting straighter, he pressed forward and dwarfed
her hands in his. He drew them to his mouth, and his lips
tickled the tips of her fingers.

Mrs. Brewster entered with a smile, and Payton sat
straighter, pulling her hands away from the warm den
of contentment.

"Mr. Lambrick, dearie. A letter's come. Forgive me
for interrupting." Mrs. Brewster left the envelope by the
edge of his glass, and he opened it immediately as Payton
looked on, wondering as to the correspondent.

It was impossible to read his face. His features
clouded, were almost guarded. She touched his arm. "Is
everything all right?"

He rose and strode to the side table. "A letter from
Anne's mother. She says that Anne has… Well, Fitzhugh
apparently tried to force his attentions on her. Her mother
doesn't know who to turn to. As the only brother Anne
has—"

"You feel you should go."

"I should prefer not to, Payton."

She offered her best smile. Just knowing he didn't
want to leave her was enough. "Shall I go along?"

"No." He bent and kissed the tip of her nose. "You stay.
I'll go faster on Storm and be back tomorrow. After all,
we have Christmas to celebrate in two days, all alone.
No foolish guests to take up our time. Besides, I don't
trust Fitzhugh. I would not want you near him if what
her mother says is true. I am sorry."

She curled her fingers around his arm and drew herself out of the chair, decidedly sad they would once again be separated just as they tried to truly commit to one another. "Take care, Jonathan. I cannot lose you." His breath troubled the hair on top of her head, and she trembled at the feelings the gesture invoked. One day would be too long, but her question concerning her father could wait. He had enough on his mind.

His hands dug into her arms, and he leaned back and stared. "Nor I you, my darling."

# Chapter 11

An hour later as he left the property, he spied Payton flying over the lands, her hair whipping her face. With her breeches on, no one would recognize her as a woman, save for the hair. His heart filled with love, and he nearly whirled around and returned to her, forgetting Anne entirely. But Lady Newbury would not have summoned him if she had not needed him. Duty called.

Would he and Payton never truly be husband and wife?

Storm roared beneath him and over the highway toward the Newbury Estate just outside of London. The animal's hooves pounded the ground in rhythm to Jonathan's heart. He feared for Anne, the way she maneuvered herself into the paths of spineless young men with no thoughts to protecting her, only of obtaining what they might from her. As her only brother, he took it upon himself, as he had for Alithea, to keep her safe and out of the way of such fops.

\* \* \*

A storm churned strong before Payton and Winter could retrace their path to Kent Hall. Wet hair plastered her cheeks, and her breeches stuck to her legs, causing them to itch. She pushed back her hair and pulled hard on Winter's reins. Steering into the wind, the cold penetrated even the hearty leather clothes.

Hearing pounding hooves behind her, she expected to turn around and spy Jonathan on Storm. But all she saw was a hand with a club.

Payton shook her head to clear it. Where was she? Rain no longer pummeled her; she could feel sun on her skin. A bag covered her face and her hands were twisted together within restraints. Someone grabbed for her ankles and she kicked hard. But raw strength overpowered her and ropes soon ensnared her feet, as well.

Hours passed as she grew colder and more frightened. Who would want to hurt her?

A door closed and a familiar voice penetrated her haze. "Well, he did it. The entire charade was for his guests, but he did it. He is rid of the snip."

Now another man spoke. "Whittard, I find it hard to believe Jonathan Lambrick ever married her in the first place. Why would he?"

"To protect her from me. Then he understood just what the marriage would mean to 'is position, and he got hold of me quick enough. She can go home with me and the missus and we'll find her work. I owe that much to my poor, dead brother."

Her uncle? Why would Jonathan engage her uncle? She struggled but the bindings tightened.

"Lambrick feared she might find her way back to Kent, so he had us take her. She won't be goin' back home after we cross enough ground. Our place is near the sea. Maybe she can earn her keep as a barmaid. She'd better. I don't want no parasites livin' off me."

Payton shuddered. He intended to keep her? Where was Jonathan? She did not believe for one minute he had planned this.

Though the Newbury estate had run down considerably after Colin Newbury's death, Jonathan recognized that Anne did her best to maintain it. Grateful the property had not been entailed on a male heir, he believed Anne had enough to support her and her ailing mother in comfort. He could still imagine the grounds as they had been just a few years ago, with gentle sloping meadows full of the finest horses.

He reached for Anne's hand and tried to read her face. "Are you all right?"

"Oh, Jonathan. I am humiliated for Mother bringing you out on a fool's errand." She strolled into the parlor, where hot tea awaited them. She poured out and passed him a cup.

His hand wrapped about the dainty china. This was beginning to feel like a social visit. "But her letter?"

Her face clouded and she looked him in the eye as he rose. "Mother isn't well, Jonathan. She misunderstood what I told her about Wallace. He never… Well, she shouldn't have alarmed you."

Jonathan leaned back and shook his head. "But her letter." He rose from the chair.

"Mother hears things. Sees people when they aren't even there. She told me the other evening she had spoken with father, and he's been dead for years. I am truly sorry she brought you on a fool's errand. Go home. I have no doubt Payton needs you more than I."

He would like to speak with her mother, but Anne was

correct in saying that he belonged at home with Payton.
Signaling for his coat, he turned on his heel.

The dusty hood came off Payton's head long enough
for her to be fed a stale piece of bread and some water. A
man knelt in front of her as she thought of escape. Though
she mentally devised ways to kick him as he fed her, she
waited. Kicking him now would throw her off balance
and she might fall into him. No telling what might happen if she were to fall against those brawny arms. She
shuddered and tears welled but with courage enough she
spit bread into the man's face. "Where am I?"

As he swiped at the crumbs, she heard a bellowing
voice enter the room. "Here now. What's that all about?
Why are you actin' foul to my wife's brother? He was
just helpin' you to have a bite."

"Uncle?"

His arms spread wide, but his smile soured her stomach. "My own precious little niece. My own flesh and
blood." His teeth oozed dark brown in the creases and
she wished he would close his mouth or turn away.

"What am I doing here, Uncle?"

"I've come to take ya home, child. Home where ya
belong. The missus is fixin' a room for ya as we speak.
Sorry I wasn't in time to protect you from that Lambrick
fella. But be assured he won't find ya where we're goin'."

"But we're married, Uncle. I am Mrs. Jonathan Lambrick."

"Never fear. I already talked to Miss Anne Newbury.
Ran into her at the inn. She explained the whole thing."

"Anne? What do you mean you spoke with Anne?"

"We'll get the marriage annulled. You wait an' see."

He couldn't do that, could he? She was Jonathan's true
and legal bride. No one could separate them. "I don't want

it annulled." And what was he talking about Anne? She couldn't have anything to do with her uncle!

"Don't speak unless you're spoken to!"

She twisted her head away when he raised his hand, but she felt the brunt of his wrath in his words. Turning onto her side, she cried until no more tears came. *Oh, Jonathan, where are you?*

"She don't even have a dress. What am I supposed to do with her? Why not let her work in the stable with you?"

Edgar's wife paced the floor with Payton tied to a chair. Rusted pans hung on a metal spike over the fire and benches sat astride a long wooden table propped up by a slab of wood on one corner. Her aunt, if she were in fact even married to Uncle Edgar, walked hunched over with a slight limp. Her hair fell in long strings of dirty brown and her teeth were worse than Edgar's. She made no attempt to smile at Payton.

Payton struggled against the ropes and tried to spit the rag from her mouth. She could taste dirt and filth. If only she could free herself. She looked from her uncle to her aunt, and her stomach churned. His red nose reminded her of the man who used to feed her father's dogs when he was away in town. She had been warned to stay away from the man. He had been taken with too much drink, and she recognized the same trait in her uncle.

He plucked at her leather jacket and then removed the rag. "She can muck out stalls. The breeches'll be good for that."

She exercised her jaw until the muscles relaxed the slightest bit. Sore and tired, she tried to force her mouth to work. "What did you do with Winter? Is she all right?"

"She brought a pretty penny at auction this mornin'. You won't be needin' a mount like her now, will ya?"

He sold Winter? He had no right. Winter belonged to her, to Jonathan. "My husband will be searching for me. He'll find you."

His hands danced before her face and came, at last, to rest on a pistol at his side. "He won't want to be arguin' with me, little miss. If he takes it into his head to fight, I'll put him under the ground with one shot. If you care about that man, you should be prayin' he keeps his distance."

She had been praying since she was taken from Kent. Praying Jonathan would find her, praying he would be safe, praying God would see to it her uncle left her alone.

"After she eats, put the rag back in her mouth." He barked orders like she imagined a military man might.

"You don't expect me to be feedin' her! You can do it yourself. I ain't your servant, Edgar."

He backhanded the woman, and she landed with a plop on her rump. "You'll do as you're told or you'll be muckin' the stalls and the pretty miss here'll be the new mistress of my house. You get my meanin'?" His laugh filled the room and then he was gone.

Payton understood all too well. She shriveled against the chair and closed her eyes.

"I don't know what he 'spects me to feed you, but I guess you'll have to eat somethin'." She fished around an old barrel and pulled out an apple and a piece of cheese with a bit of mold on the edges.

Payton shook her head. "Just water, please. I'm not particularly hungry."

"Well then, if the old man asks, you tell him I offered. I don't care if you starve to death. You've already been more trouble than you're worth. Don't know how much he 'spects to get fer ya, but it ain't enough in my book."

"Has no one seen her, then?" Jonathan paced the floor of the stable, his boots bruising the straw with each step. He slammed his gloves on the table, and his face broiled hotter every minute. He could almost picture his scar raised and red, reminding him how he got it in the first place.

"No, sir. Her riding clothes are gone and so is Winter. They never returned."

He stopped pacing, faced Mr. Kenny and exhaled sharply. "If she had been thrown, Winter would have come back to the stable."

"Yessir. Should I saddle Storm again, Mr. Lambrick?"

"No. Let him rest. Saddle Templar." He retrieved his gloves and donned his jacket once again. "I'll make a complete turn about the property. Don't expect me until late. If she should return, keep her here. Don't let her go out hunting for me. Understood?"

"Certainly. But wouldn't you like me to ride with you?"

He took in Kenny's demeanor. The man had seen many years managing the stables. His hands were gnarled with experience and the skin was pulled tight across his swollen joints. His steps had grown slow and, although he did the master's bidding without complaint, Jonathan recognized he was in pain. "No, but I thank you for the offer."

Mrs. Brewster entered the stable, surprising him. She stepped forward, and he soaked in the compassion from behind the tired old eyes. He hadn't realized how his staff had aged. Once Payton was found, he would have to make arrangements for younger servants to do the heavy work at Kent Hall while preserving the present staff's dignity.

"Sir," Mrs. Brewster said, "she would not have left of her own accord. I know Pay—Mrs. Lambrick. She has a heart for you and no one else."

He thought for a moment, patting her hand, and searched for an answer. "So you think I am remembering Alithea?"

"Are you not?"

"No, I am not." He leaned down and pecked her cheek. "But I appreciate your caring." One day he would find a way to repay all of her kindnesses to him since he had been a child at her kitchen table. For now, he had to ride.

Mr. Kenny clapped a hand on his shoulder. "Sir, no one would dare harm Mrs. Lambrick. No one would be so foolhardy, sir."

"I have no doubt you are right." He tried to smile, but a twisted grimace was all he could muster and his insides churned with fear for her.

Payton strained to adjust her eyes to the dark room they'd thrown her into. A storage room? What good would it do for her uncle and aunt to have kidnapped her? What might they do for a living? A shudder rippled through her. She'd heard of girls disappearing. What happened to them? She had to find a way out of here.

Twisting for a better view, she scanned the shelves above her head. Tins and boxes of food lined the straight boards and a crock of something greasy rested on the floor next to her pallet. An iron hook hung over the wooden candle holder, and she thought perhaps she could use it as a weapon if necessary. Mouse and spider droppings speckled the bottom shelf, where a flour sack jammed against the wall. Her stomach growled, and she reached for a piece of bread off one of the platters, but she couldn't lift her hand high enough with the restraints tugging down. She licked her lips and sagged onto the pallet once again. Pulling up her feet, she leaned her arms against her knees until her chin came to rest on the back of her hands. How would she escape this place?

A door banged shut in the other room, and she heard voices.

"Things has changed."

The woman's husky voice chimed in. "What do you mean? Ain't the captain o' the ship going to buy her now?"

"He says he don't want no trouble. I can't get no one to take 'er off our hands. So we're goin' ta make the master pay for her."

"You think he will?"

Her uncle's voice overpowered the woman he said was her aunt, and Payton cringed. "Shut up! If he don't, I'll just throw 'er in the sea. No one'll be the wiser."

More foul words and a loud smack. The woman sniffled. "What was that for?"

"Ya feed the brat?"

She heard what she thought was the woman scuffling over the floor toward the door leading into the pantry. "I give 'er a crumb o' bread. That's good enough. We don't have no extra to be handin' out like a charity." More smarmy comments.

"If we don't keep 'er healthy, she'll tell Lambrick and he'll be huntin' us down when this is over. We need ta get the money and head for the northland. He'll not think to look there."

"Shh."

"Don't shush me, woman."

"She might hear. Keep yer voice down. You don't want him comin' after us. Maybe he'll pay and leave us be."

Footsteps to the door. A thin thread of light blossomed as the door cracked open. Payton closed her eyes, leaned against the shelf and feigned sleep. Let them think she hadn't heard. "Nah. She's sleepin' all right. I'm goin' to the inn and sendin' Bobby with the letter. He'll leave it for Lambrick and we'll see what he does."

"Has he any idea where we live?"

"None."

The woman's voice sounded anxious. "What if he doesn't want 'er back? After all, he didn't marry for love or money."

"He better want 'er back or she's a dead woman. She may be a dead woman anyway. If there's any chance he could connect us to her... The man has a temper. I heard from a lady he was the one killed his first wife. That fancy lady he's always with is the woman's sister. She figured she'd be the new mistress of Kent 'til this chit come along. Interestin' prospect, what?"

The woman started laughing. "Well then, we take the money and save 'im the effort with wife number two and the fancy lady can have 'im after all."

Payton shivered. What if they were right and Jonathan did perceive this as a way out of the marriage? But he couldn't have been acting. He loved her. She pulled the flour sack they had given her about her shoulders and cried herself to sleep.

Jonathan rounded the stable in time to spy a man in a brown cape jump on his horse and ride away as though evil himself trailed him. He quickened his pace where outside the door Clarisse held an envelope. "What did that man want?"

She held out her hand. "A letter, sir. Addressed to you."
He tore the envelope open.

*She ain't worth much money, is what I often said.*
*But if you don't pay it, she'll be nothing but dead.*
*You got two days to leave five thousand pounds*
*in the poor box at St. Peter's Church in Colches-*
*ter at exactly six o'clock in the evening. If anyone*
*comes with you, she dies. Once the money is in*
*the box, turn around and look for the large horse*
*chestnut tree. Do not look back at the church.*
*There you will find directions to the young miss.*
*Do exactly as this letter says or she dies.*

Jonathan reread the letter until it was nothing more
than a crumpled mess. He then strode through the door.
Just inside, he slammed his hand on the wooden table and
sent the bowl of flowers sailing over the floor. Mrs. Brewster struggled to catch the large silver urn but missed.

"Emily!"

"Right behind you, dearie."

"I'll be in my room for the remainder of the evening.
Tell Mr. Kenny to have my mount ready first thing in
the morning."

"What are you planning to do?"

"I'm planning to get Payton back if I have to turn Colchester upside down."

"Do you know where she is?"

"No. They want money to tell me, but if I pay them,
I'll never see her again. They won't let her live."

"Why is that?"

"Because I will hunt them down like the dogs they are
and kill them. And they know it."

# Chapter 12

Weary of feeling sorry for herself, Payton pulled her shoulders back, lifted her chin and enjoyed an unusual moment of confidence. She had heard the woman mention Colchester earlier. That wasn't a long ride from Kent Park. Would she be able to find her way home before they realized she was gone?

She gazed past the metal hook and noticed a small table filled with tools. If only she could locate a knife, a saw or any other instrument to cut herself loose. She scooted on her rump across the floor and in front of the table. Whenever she tried to reach out, the ropes around her ankles pulled tighter, like a noose. Pushing up on her knees as far as she could before the pain became unbearable, she spied only a file and some wooden boxes atop the table. She stretched up but couldn't quite reach. Within seconds the ropes had tightened around her ankles and cut against her skin. Still, just a bit more and she would be able to bring down the file. She nudged the table. Nudged it again. She heard the file scraping closer to the edge. Another bump with her shoulder.

One more shove and down it came with a thud, the point barely missing her leg.

Her hands shook as they closed over it, and she returned to the other side of the room by inching her way along. *I can do this.*

Once on the dirty straw she leaned against the wall to support her shoulder and provide her feet a break from the pain. She wedged the file behind her hands and commenced to grate the rough edge against the ropes on her wrists. The ropes on her ankles tightened again and she winced. Pain shot through her until she cried out, tears flowing.

"Hey, in there. Keep it down. Ain't no one out here wants ta hear ya cryin'."

She gasped. Would they hear her sawing? Taking more care, she began again, one scrape at a time. Too often she missed the rope and rubbed her skin raw. Warm and sticky blood coursed over her. She sucked in her breath. *Don't cry out.*

Hours passed, and she continued to work a few minutes and then give her hand a break. But the throbbing overwhelmed her so she knew if she didn't continue, she never would be able to finish. Footsteps growing fainter and a door closing told her both her captors had vacated the building. She seized the opportunity to cry out until the rope on her wrists gave way.

Releasing her ankles was much easier. They immediately popped loose and she stretched her legs. How good it felt. She stared at the rope burns around her ankles and wrists and gagged. Blood spattered her feet, her hands and the straw around her. Knowing she might only have minutes until they returned, she opened the door slowly, stared into the other room, saw no one and slipped across the floor. She palmed a piece of bread from the table and moved to the door. A quick peek out the window told her they were nowhere in sight.

When she rounded the corner and saw Edgar and his wife, her heart rate spiraled. In an instant, they looked in her direction and she ran until there was no breath left in her body. A glance behind showed her they had not been able to keep up with her or hadn't recognized it as her in the first place. She slowed for a minute, bent at the waist, hands on her knees, the air coming in slow, deep gasps.

"Hey there, boy." A constable shouted at her and she spun on her foot and fled. Jumping onto a cart headed in the opposite direction, she snuggled into the straw and sighed. Perhaps they were headed toward Kent Park. She would know soon enough.

She had fallen asleep and it was now pitch-black. She smelled the sea. Could she be near the coast? Raising her head, she looked in time to see a sloop anchored off the water. As she raised her head to get a better idea of her surroundings, the driver of the cart shrieked at her, and she dropped over the side onto the road.

Where could she hide? The ship. If she hid on board until assured they hadn't followed her, she might be able to catch a ride back to Kent Park. The danger of such a plan frightened her. Perhaps a church. They would hide her until they could send her home. But what if they didn't believe her story? The ship was still her best choice. No one would search for her there.

Tired and hungry, she fled in the dark until she was alongside the ship's gangway. No one in attendance convinced her it was safe to sneak aboard. She padded softly over the wet boards, leaving behind a trail of blood, but she didn't care. She wanted safety and this seemed a logical option. Her feet burned and her hands, rubbed raw from the cutting, stung. She shrank from the cold, but managed to snatch a dirty cap from the deck. Her heart filled her chest with throbs she couldn't control. A quick glance around took her to a fold of canvas. Shivering from the cold, she tucked her hair under the cap, crawled under, and in no time at all, she slept.

Jonathan's heart pressed into his chest. Would whoever had taken Payton make good on the threat and kill her? His noble stand crumbled as he thought of her alone, wondering why he didn't save her. He would pay. Whatever they wanted. All they had to do was just bring Payton back. He wasted no more time considering what they might do.

The next morning Jonathan waited in the office to speak with his solicitor and arrange for the money. The man wasn't overpaid, that was certain. The frugal appearance of the office said he either took care with money or was outright stingy. He had known Joseph Worley for nine years and knew he wasn't stingy.

With hand already extended, Worley entered the room. "Mr. Lambrick, what brings you to Colchester?"

Jonathan explained the best he could, though his voice rose and fell in sharp gasps that left him choking for more air. Just thinking about Payton's safety sent coils of pain stretching through him.

"And what makes you think they'll return her even if you pay?"

His hands formed fists on his thighs. "The person must know me and if he does, he also understands I will kill him if she is hurt in any way." *Forgive me, Lord, but I have to find Payton...alive.*

"As your counsel, I must say, I cannot be certain we will be able to have this readied for your time schedule."

Jonathan reached across the desk and grabbed Worley by his waistcoat, twisting the brocade fabric into a knot. "Make no mistake. You will have the money I need—on time."

"See here, Cap'n. We got us a stowaway." The sail lifted and exposed Payton. She scuttled back on her haunches and folded her arms over her face. "A boy, sir. What'll we do with 'im?"

"Haul him over the side. We'll find out how well he swims." The captain laughed aloud, leaving no doubt he meant business.

"No! Please! I can't swim." Payton's hands clutched at the filthy swabbie who'd hauled her up.

The captain strolled over and clipped Payton under the chin while the man in the worn striped shirt looked on and smiled. "Well, you can't very well work off your stay. You're too scrawny for a cabin boy."

*Thank You, God. They think I'm a boy.* "I—I'll just leave. Let me go, please." She spun on her heel for a quick retreat.

But the captain was too quick. He stepped closer and recognition crossed his face. He reached out and yanked at the front of her jacket.

A smell stung her nostrils as she fought with him.

Then the captain turned her over to the man with the smelly shirt and no tooth in front. Another man, younger, joined them.

"Please. I'm not who you think. The name is Payton Whittard...Lambrick."

The captain spoke before the others. "See here. I told Whittard I wanted no part of this plan. Why did he send you here?" Three sets of eyes stared at her, waiting for an answer.

She struggled to make sense of his words. He knew Uncle Edgar? "He didn't send me, sir. I needed somewhere safe to go and hide until I could return home. If you'll just let me leave, I'll find a way back. But, please, don't take me back to Whittard's cottage."

The man raked her from head to toe. "I must say, you are a bit weak but with the right clothes and attention, you might make a fine addition for the crew to enjoy."

She gasped. "Who are you?"

The other man licked his lips and hissed through a great gap in his teeth. "He's the captain, missy. Captain Jeremiah Dooley."

"Then, sir, I take you for a gentleman."

The three men roared louder than lions, each of them grinning wide. The captain slapped his knee. "A gentleman? Did you hear that, boys?"

Payton gazed around the men and saw movement. She realized the sloop rocked on the water. They were already out to sea.

Suddenly she felt the wedge of bread coming up her throat. She turned her head and relieved herself.

Jonathan's long strides brought him close to St. Peter's Church. He looked around for any sign of Payton but kept to the task at hand. Bring her back alive. Five thousand pounds or no five thousand pounds, Payton must be returned to him. Too late he had realized how much she meant to him. He should have protected her long before this.

Out of the corner of his eye, he thought he recognized

a man. He did. Edgar Whittard doing his best to blend
into the evening bustle of people in the throes of shopping and selling; Jonathan turned for a better look. The
man had disappeared into the crowd. If he was the man
behind the ransom, Jonathan would see to it he soon
breathed his last.

For now, he entered the church and headed for the poor
box. Inside, he placed the satchel of pound notes. He retraced his steps outside and strode straight to the back
of the building. Slipping inside, he made his way slowly
through the dark to the front, where he waited in a small
vestibule for the mangy dog who had Payton.

Minutes passed, and no one entered. When he thought
perhaps this had been a fool's errand, he heard heavy
footsteps. He opened the door a crack and watched. As
Edgar Whittard forced open the poor box, Jonathan overpowered him. "Where is Payton?"

"Don't know what yer talkin' about."

With his arm wrapped about Edgar's neck, he tightened his grip until the man's eyes bulged. "You'll tell me
now or I'll break your neck."

"Don't know. Don't know," he croaked the words. "Let
go and I'll tell ya what I heard."

Jonathan loosened his grip just a mite, barely enough
for Whittard to take shallow breaths. "Go on. Tell me!"

"I seen her…come into town disguised like a man on a
great…beast of a horse. Ridin' like the wind. She met up
with this woman…fancy lady. I overheard them talkin'.
They planned to get money from the master of Kent…
they said." Whittard pulled at Jonathan's hands, and Jonathan loosened the tension slightly. Air rushed through
Whittard's lips. "Back off. I can't breathe."

Jonathan lessened the grasp around Whittard's

throat, though he longed to continue to squeeze. "Don't try anything."

"Payton was sailing on a ship for Dorset and the other lady was gettin' the money and then meetin' up with her somewhere on the southern coast of the county. They didn't know I was listenin' but I was and I figured ta get the money before they did. So I watched the church and beat 'em in here. That's the truth. All I know."

"You're lying!"

"My wife be dead if I'm lyin'. The girl's no good, I tell ya. She and the high fallutin' lady, Newcome or some name like that, are just out fer yer money."

Jonathan released him. Not again. How could he have been fooled again? No. She wouldn't do what her uncle claimed. He might believe Anne could be a party to this. She'd do anything to get her hands on the money needed to improve Newbury, but not Payton. She loved him. He was sure. And he…loved her.

"I'm sorry I can't tell ya more about her, but I don't know nothin'."

"Ahh, so noble. Yet you would have taken my money quickly enough."

"I admit. I would that. My wife and me've seen hard times. I was hopin' to have Payton come work for us, that's all. If you want to find out what happened to my niece, you should talk to that fancy woman if she's still in town."

"I intend to do just that." As he retrieved the satchel, Whittard whirled for escape. Before Jonathan could stop him, Whittard ran through the church and out the back.

In a few minutes, he was back on Templar and tearing through Colchester. Passing the docks, he stopped and sighed. A sloop sliced through the waves. To take a trip with Payton on that magnificent ship, leaving England behind. England and all the misery he'd grown to know as his intimate companion. Right now, he wanted nothing more than home; hopefully, Payton would be waiting there.

Payton's eyes welled with tears. Here she sat, the men staring at her. She scrambled to her feet and planted her hands on her hips, but the swaying of the ship sent her back to the rail, where she retched until her stomach calmed. All day she wondered what they would finally do with her. Now, the captain eyed her with cold determination.

"She needs to leave." The captain shouted orders, and Payton shivered against the cold.

"What'll we do? Throw her over?"

"You idiot! Not in this water. She'd freeze as soon as she hit."

"So? What's it t'us?"

Captain Dooley rubbed his chin and stared at her as if she were a prize turkey. She clutched her arms across her chest and stumbled back.

"T'would solve the problem. No, we can't. Her folks'll hunt us down. I'm not one looking for trouble. I've enough chasing me. We'll just turn around and drop her over the side."

She took a step back, but the rail stopped her. "What are you going to do? You said I'd freeze in the water!"

"Not what I would be disposed to do, pretty miss, if you stayed aboard." His eyes twinkled, and she sucked back a shaky breath. "I s'pose there's a bit of that gentleman in me, after all. You'll have but a short swim."

She quivered under the leather jacket and longed to collapse onto the deck and cry, but she wouldn't allow them the pleasure of her fear.

"You can't throw me over."

"You would rather stay and be entertainment for my men?"

*Dear God. Help me out of here. I will do whatever You say, but please, help me find my way home.* Payton drew up and brushed at her clothes. "Very well. Jonah did it, so shall I."

Captain Dooley held out his hand. "We'll take you as close as we can, but I'll not drop anchor. You'll have a ways to swim." He tossed a cloak to her and insisted she warm as much as possible before the plunge. "Let me fetch you a bite to eat for strength. The best I can do, miss. I won't find myself in trouble for your running off."

# Chapter 13

How could he rest when Payton was in danger? *God, I know I've not been a praying man, but I need You with me. I must find her. This isn't her fault and she deserves better. Keep her safe. And please help me.*

Templar pulled alongside the stable and Jonathan jumped to the ground before the animal fully stopped. "Any sign of Payton?"

"No, sir. None."

"Take care of Templar."

"You haven't found her, either, sir?"

"No." He kicked at a rock on the ground and knew he would never rest until he found Payton. "Get Storm ready. I'll leave again in two hours." He hated to ride his best horses so hard, but what choice did he have? Templar and Storm were the strongest horseflesh in the county.

Thus far the key to all of Payton's troubles had been

Edgar Whittard. Had Anne truly been involved also? He would learn the truth. One way or the other. He had to learn what happened to her.

Swirling, dirty water filled her ears, her eyes and her mouth as she fought to stay afloat. Her teeth clacked together so hard, she was afraid they might break. Not much farther. The captain had been as good as his word and had brought the sloop around as closely as possible. She had been in the water less than ten minutes with naught but a piece of wood to keep her from sinking. She spied faint lights and heard the noise of a busy dock. Would she be safe coming out of the water in this part of town? No choice. The need to get warm, and fast, spurred her on.

Jonathan. She wanted Jonathan. He could not have been part of this. Of that she was sure. But who might assist her, believe her story? The church? Could she find her way to the church before Edgar found her? She wished she'd chosen the church earlier.

Cold, dark water continued to tug at her legs and arms and pulled at her heavy, wet clothes. In an instant, the chill overcame her and she bobbed under as everything grew black.

Voices flowed in and out of her head. A woman's voice, a man's. She tried to speak, but the words drifted and distorted through her senses.

"Where are you from, dearie? Can we fetch family for ya'?"

The man's voice floated on more brutal terms. "Maybe she's a runaway. A kid. How about if she works for us? Could give you a break from time to time, Emma."

Payton coughed up water and pulled herself to a sitting position. "I have family in town," she lied. "I'll be fine."

"Suit yerself." The woman, draped in scraps that barely covered her ample body, watched as the man walked away. He had a proper hat on his head, but his jacket, frayed and dirty, was at least two sizes too small.

In a threatening voice, he shouted over his shoulder, "Back to work, Emma Jean. I don't pay you to sit on yer arse."

"Here." Emma offered a piece of something brown to Payton and she accepted it warily, hunger the deciding factor. "You should find your folks. If he comes back and you're still here…"

"Thank you." She ate the doughy substance and surveyed her surroundings for any sign of familiarity. The poorest part of town winked at her like a beacon. After walking for little more than half an hour, she recognized her uncle's street. A carriage, unlikely in this area, rumbled over the cobblestones, leaving the avenue. When it drew near her, she heard a woman's voice. "Payton? Is that you? Driver, stop!" Anne Newbury leaned from the carriage.

"Miss Newbury. Oh, Anne. Please help me." Within seconds, Payton leaned against double cushions and had a robe tucked about her. "Please take me home."

Anne patted her hand. "You can't go home like this. Driver, back to Newbury immediately." Payton watched a rusty stain coil about Anne's white glove.

"Are you all right? Did you harm yourself?" Payton asked.

"Nothing for you to worry about, dear. Get some sleep if you can."

Payton's eyes closed. "But I want Jonathan."

"Tomorrow, after we've taken care to make you strong. Right now, you need sleep and Newbury is closer than Kent. I'll see that Jonathan gets word."

Storm's hooves crackled against the frosty leaves as horse and rider pounded the open highway to Colchester. Jonathan, after being talked into some hot broth and a short rest before departing, was refreshed enough to see this to the end. Storm snorted and reared when they jumped a fallen branch in the road, but Jonathan held tight. Absolutely no way had Payton been involved in this blackmail. This smelled of Edgar Whittard. Was he bright enough to plan such an intricate plot by himself? Or had Whittard found help? Surely not Anne. Not after the history of the families, yet, she seemed the only likely one who might have had a part in Payton's abduction. He didn't want to believe it.

The sun had set quickly and it grew more difficult to see the way.

"Whoa, boy. We're all right. Easy now." If only he could convince himself of the same advice. *Whoa, boy, yourself. It's all going to be all right. Take it an hour at a time until you discover her whereabouts.* With heart hammering, his chest ached with each bout of puffing and panting in the rush to discover Payton. Now atop Storm, he couldn't relax a measure.

Stars soon sparkled in a clear sky, creating an easier journey than would have been expected. As Jonathan drew near Colchester, he saw the first faint light of dawn appear on the horizon. Reining Storm in, he guided them slowly toward the center of town. After asking around, he discovered Edgar's dwelling situated five streets closer to the docks.

Once next to the entrance of the run-down shamble

of a cottage, he leaped off the horse's back and landed hard on his knee. Bending to rub it, he stared at the door to the Whittards'.

Tethering Storm, he spun on his heel and determined how to approach Whittard. In spite of the pain, he covered the walk in two strides. Planting himself firmly in front, he pounded on the door, not caring whether he disturbed the owners on either side. Nothing. When he rapped again, the door gave under his hand and he pressed forward.

"Whittard?" He entered, his eyes adjusting to the lack of light. He tripped over something on the floor and bent to see what it was. "Man! What happened to you?" He nudged the man's body. Fat legs stuck into the room. An old woman in worse condition lay sprawled across the floor. Finally cheated the wrong man, no doubt. Or perhaps the wrong woman?

With the possibility of Anne's involvement, Jonathan hurriedly let himself out and retrieved Storm's reins. With a groan, he hoisted his leg over the animal's back and headed out of town, straight to Newbury.

Payton leaned against Anne as they both wobbled up the stairs.

"Lynette! Bring fresh linens. And hurry, foolish girl!"

Anne's words were harsh. She obviously didn't care a whit about the servants. Perhaps she worried about Payton. Perhaps not.

"We'll have you settled soon. Trust me, Payton. I shall take care of you."

Within the hour, Payton snuggled into a bed with warm, soft covers that slipped against her like a second skin; the maidservant hovered for any sign of a request.

Payton gazed into the frightened face and said, "Thank you for your care. You've been so kind."

The girl's eyes bugged as she curtseyed and bobbed unnaturally in a manner Payton assumed she must do on a daily basis. "Well, I… Thank you…miss. You need anything, just ring the bell, and I'll come runnin'."

She barely spoke the words before Payton's eyes closed. "The name is…Mrs. Lambrick, Lynette."

Later, when the door opened quietly, she heard, "I think she's awake, mum."

"You are not paid to think, Lynette."

Payton struggled through the fog of heavy sleep and wondered at Anne's disagreeable nature. She hated seeing that side of her but assumed it was out of concern. "Anne, thank you for all your help, but I want to go back to Kent."

"Nonsense. You're in no condition. Here now, my physician came while you were sleeping. He left this powder for you. He said you would sleep the sleep of the dead. No arguing. Take it at once." Anne took a glass from the stand, filled it with water and added the powder. "You will sleep most of the morning and then, if you're well, I'll take you home."

Payton accepted the glass and finished most of it. "Thank you. Jonathan and I both thank you."

"I'll bring up a tray in a few minutes if you're still awake. No one else shall care for you from now on."

"But Lynette is goodness itself."

Anne shook her head. "I am family, dear. I'll see to your needs."

Payton's sleep came quickly but with distress. She awoke time and again to the sound of anxious noises. Jonathan? Did she hear his deep, warm voice? "Jonathan? Is that you?"

She couldn't fight her sleep-filled eyes.

* * *

Jonathan broached no nonsense. "But why would she leave?"

"I told you, Jonathan. I met Mr. Whittard at a carriage stop. He acted so strangely. Then, he divulged Payton's plan to try and secure enough money to run away. He said the entire plot with him started as her idea. She did not want to have to stay at Kent. I have no way of knowing how she contacted him. A woman plotting a man's demise is foreign to my nature. She was to pay Whittard half of what she collected. Such betrayal, Jonathan."

He rose and moved to the fireplace mantle, where he stood a long while before speaking. "The time has come for you to know about Alithea."

"Alithea? We were speaking of Payton Whittard. Jonathan, why do you frown so, and why are you bringing up my dead sister?"

Why indeed? Did he believe all women contrived to plot against him? Alithea? Payton? He stared long at Anne's face, her features unyielding. He could trust no one. "You need to be made aware of what happened the night Alithea ran away."

"Jonathan, I know what happened."

He drew his chair closer to her. "No, but before this day is over, you will. Perhaps then, we can be completely open with one another."

Payton stumbled to the top of the stairs. When she leaned against the rail, it wobbled under her hand. Jonathan had been correct in saying that Newbury needed a man's attention. And his money.

Surely she had heard Jonathan's voice. No other man's words stirred her heart so. It had to be him. Why didn't he come to her? All she owned in the world she would gladly give away for one kind word from Jonathan.

"Payton, what are you doing out of bed?" Anne gripped her around the shoulders and steered her toward the guest quarters.

"Jonathan's here?"

"No, dear. Why do you ask?"

No one would convince her otherwise. "But I heard him."

Anne's grasp pulled her away from the stairs. "That must be from the laudanum Dr. Blakely gave you. Payton, dear, you must get your rest if you are to go home. Come back to your room."

Anne prepared another drink and offered it to her. Payton took only enough to dampen her dry, cracked lips.

Jonathan paced the great hall, waiting for Anne to return. She had taken the news of Alithea so calmly. Did she believe him? Fancy him crazy? Or had she known all along that Alithea only cared about his wealth?

Anne entered, freshly dressed for dinner in a gown better suited to a ball than a family meal. "I do hope you will stay and eat before you start your search again." Her hand reached out and stroked his shoulder.

He stepped away, uncomfortable at her familiarity. Changing the subject, he said, "Is your mother all right? I had no idea she had taken to her bed. I am sorry to hear it."

"She's fine. A bit restless, perhaps, but that is to be expected now that she cannot get around easily. If only she... Well, that matters not."

He indicated the stairwell. "Would she be up to seeing a visitor?"

"Oh, my, no. She barely speaks anymore and I would

not want to embarrass her. Perhaps another time, Jonathan. I don't know how I will ever tell her about Alithea or if I even should." She leaned into him and buried her face in his chest. "It might have been me, Jonathan. You know I loved you from the beginning."

"Anne, please."

"Oh, Jonathan."

"As much as I would like to stay and have dinner with you, I must go. Payton is out there, and I have to find her. She's all alone, Anne. And I cannot believe she was part of Edgar Whittard's plan in spite of what you've told me."

Anne pushed him from her. Her face contorted. "You are a fool! You were a fool with Alithea and you're a fool with Payton. I was in love with you, Jonathan. Not Alithea. Not Payton! I have always been here for you. And what do I get? I am pushed aside time and again." She drew a handkerchief to her eyes. "What must I do to make you see me? Here. Waiting."

He recalled numerous occasions when she had put herself between him and Alithea, between him and Payton. Was she in earnest that she loved him? He looked for his coat; he must leave. He would come back and deal with Anne later.

"I never meant to hurt you, Anne. If I have, forgive me. But I will find Payton before harm comes to her." His feet took him past the decaying tapestry that adorned the hallway. Past the crumbling foundation in the entrance. Past the door, which hung askance. How far would Anne go to see Newbury restored?

# Chapter 14

Ten days passed with no word from Payton. Jonathan sat alone in his library, where he now spent the bulk of his time. His hand reached up and brushed at the uncharacteristic facial hair. His eyes ached when he tried to read; his lips burned from the dryness. He grabbed the water on his desk and downed it in one gulp, but still dry sand filled his mouth. The musty books, no doubt. He gazed about at the shelves and made a mental note to arrange for Clarisse to dust them. Cleanse the entire hall from all the deception.

He started when he heard a noise. "Supper, sir?"

"Go away, Emily."

"But, sir."

"I'm not hungry!" The quiet enveloped him again. Emily had not been able to entice him with his favorite foods, and he knew he'd grown gaunt. But why should he care? There was no one for whom it would make a differ-

ence. Anne had called, but he'd sent her away. He did not
desire guests. Not even work lured him from the house.

"Mr. Lambrick, Mr. Walmsley and Mr. Cole have been
here two times this week. They have asked for your help.
Your tenants, sir."

"Let them be hanged for all I care. Leave. I'm tired."

His parents gone. Alithea gone, and now Payton.
Where was she? If only he thought she was happy. And
safe. But he did not believe for one minute Payton had
been part of a plan to cheat him. Yet Anne had been so
adamant and they had been friends for years, even before he'd married Alithea.


Payton stumbled along the hallway, mumbling and
shaking uncontrollably. Her head clouded whenever she
tried to think. Anne had told her Jonathan had been killed
by Whittard. If Jonathan had been killed, it was all her
fault. She could never return to Kent. Now there was no
reason to go back.

She retraced her steps and drew, once again, from the
glass Anne left for her on the stand; the drink made her
forget, helped her to cope with his death. *God, why has
this happened? Why did You allow it?* Her heart wrenched
inside her as she drank deeply of the cool water.

Not soon enough, she fell across the bed and gave in
as hypnotizing sleep consumed her. "Jonathan, why did
you leave me?"

When Payton awoke, she could barely force her eyes
to open. Her mouth was thick and dry. Her breathing
labored and demanding. She struggled to get out of the
bed. Those voices again. Loud, arguing. Jonathan? Not
Jonathan. Another woman. Who?

"You cannot simply leave her here like this. How will
that help us?"

"Mother, you are talking like a fool. Be patient a little longer and soon we will have it all. He was mine. If not for Alithea, Newbury would once again be respectable. But she didn't care about anything other than Kent Park and Jonathan. How very singular...and selfish. Mother, you and I will find a way."

"Anne, are you there?" What were they saying?

The door scraped open and Anne's face appeared. "It's time, Payton."

"Time?"

"Yes, dear. It's time to take you to Jonathan."

She must be dreaming. Jonathan died.

"Get dressed, Payton. I'll help you. I've had your breeches cleaned. And I recovered Winter for you. Tonight, once you've eaten, I'll have her saddled. And you can return to Jonathan."

"Jonathan's dead."

Anne's eyes filled. "Dear girl, have you been dreaming? Wherever did you get an idea like that?"

Emily shook his arm. Jonathan stared into familiar eyes, warm and inquisitive. He felt as if he had been dead for years.

"Mr. Lambrick. Jonathan. Please. If Miss Payton is out there, you cannot give up. She wouldn't want you to. Please, dearie. Look at you. Shameful, it is."

He wiped the tears away. "Emily?" The same kind eyes that had nursed him back to health so many times. Had taught him about God and family. How to live as a trusted and honorable master to those in his charge. He was disappointing her as well as his people. Her arms wrapped about him and he cried. He had not shed a tear since he was a child, but tonight, he cried. "I miss her, Emily. I miss her so much. I can't believe she could have been in on a plot to steal from me. Everything I have was hers for the asking."

"Jonathan, she would not leave you on purpose."

"Like Alithea?"

"No, foolish man. Someone has done Payton harm and you need to find out who. I don't believe for one minute it was her uncle. He doesn't have the sense of a mole. It took a keen mind to abduct Miss Payton and make up a story. Now, who could have done such a thing?"

He hoisted himself to a sitting position and wiped his face. Staring at the accusation in Emily's eyes, his mind whirled with a possibility. Wallace Fitzhugh, that's who.

Jonathan could ride this highway in his sleep. He had thought after Alithea died that he might have feelings for Anne and see her as a possible mate. But that was all in his past. The only woman he cared about for longer than he could remember was Payton. *Where are you? God, give me a plan. Help me to find her, please. Something in all of this is terribly wrong.*

The road seemed to lead straight to Newbury, as if his horse knew no other way.

He shouted for Ellery at the stable door and was surprised to see him saddling Cootis, Anne's favorite mount. "Would you look after Storm?"

"Yessir. I'll brush him and cool him down, sir."

His legs crossed the grass in haste. Anne must have a suggestion for him. Perhaps she would remember one small detail Fitzhugh might have let slip. Rounding the side of the house, he rammed into her. "Jonathan!"

He pulled her shoulders together with his hard grip. "What are you doing out here?"

She trembled at his words. "I... Ellery needed me in the stables. If you will excuse me. Mother is in the study having tea. Perhaps you could join her and I will meet you in a few minutes."

"Your mother?" Anne was acting so peculiar, and hadn't her mother taken to her bed? Curiosity and the possibility of pressing her mother for information propelled him toward the house. He stopped, pulled a hand through his hair, and addressed Anne with an unexpected wariness. "Please hurry."

When the door opened, Caroline Newbury seemed to be doing very well, indeed. Not at all as Anne had described her. "The reports of your health have been happily erroneous, madam. How do you do?"

Caroline Newbury's eyes darted from Jonathan to the door and back to Jonathan again. Almost out of breath she cried, "Jonathan, how good to see you."

"Are you all right?" She looked anything but an invalid, but she was obviously distressed at his arrival. He had heard of people taking a turn for the better, but Anne had made it sound as if her mother was merely awaiting the grim reaper.

She gestured to a chair with a shaking hand. "Please take a seat. Have some tea. Perhaps some bread and preserves. I'll call for Lynette." She turned to the bell and continued the incessant chattering until his head hurt. "Anne will be right back."

He settled into the chair, his eyes not straying from her loss of composure. "Yes. I spoke with her. I am pleased to see you doing so well. I had heard you were taken to your bed."

"The reports, alas, were true, but Dr. Blakely nursed me well and, as you can see, I am much improved. It has been a very long time, Jonathan. After all, you are a son to me, my dear."

He leaned over and pecked her cheek, then accepted

the cup of tea. "You know, I assume, that my wife, Payton, has been missing these past days? Have either of you heard from her?"

"No, Jonathan. Anne informed me of the sad circumstances. I am sorry for your loss, and that it seems she has taken the way of my dearest Alithea."

"What?" She continued to gaze beyond him, but why? "Madam, is something wrong? Are you and Anne in some sort of danger?" Fitzhugh came to his mind once again.

"Dear me, whatever makes you think that?" Her hands fluttered in her lap and the cup of tea spilled across the sleeve of her gown. "Oh, my. See how clumsy I am? Jonathan, it is difficult for two women to live alone. Anne has had to take over the duties of a man around here. One cannot trust the servants, my dear. I'm simply beside myself whenever she has to leave the house for these unpleasant duties. No doubt she'll be back before I can clean up this mess."

Jonathan rose and offered his handkerchief. "I cannot wait any longer. I had hoped she would remember anything Fitzhugh may have said about Payton that could help me to find her."

"You think Fitzhugh has done her harm?" She nodded. "He has been behaving rather peculiarly. You must ask Anne when she returns."

He marched toward the door. "I'll ask her now. No need to waste more time speculating." He shrugged against a sudden chill. "I don't know what to think, but I will learn. One way or the other. Of that you can be sure, and whoever is responsible will pay."

Caroline Newbury looked as if she might faint.

Though thrilled to be reunited with Winter, Payton could barely sit the saddle before Anne hit the animal with a crop. Payton's feet knocked about in the stirrups, which had been set too long; she hung on tight.

Anne smiled and waved as she turned Cootis back toward the stable. "Give Jonathan my best, dear sister."

Winter lurched forward. Payton turned to wave a hand but dared not let go of the grasp she had on the animal. More lightheaded than usual, she struggled to stay upright. Why did her head swirl so? She brushed at low-hanging branches that barely missed her face. Was this the way to Kent? Ellery had assured her it was, despite Anne's insisting she should ride in the other direction.

Her breathing came in sharp, hollow gasps and the motion of the horse caused a churning in her stomach. If only she could find her way back. Would Jonathan even care? He couldn't have been the one to send her away. She had been gone so long; at least, she thought she had.

Anne's arms encircled Jonathan's neck, but he brushed them off. "You could stay and visit with mother and me for a few days. You haven't paid us a lengthy visit in some time."

"I told you I'm going to Payton." Was Anne still living in the past? Their past? But they'd only been children when he'd declared his love to her. Only children.

"Payton! Payton! Jonathan when will you stop overlooking the love right in front of you?"

She still thought… No. "We've been over this. I am married, Anne. And I love my wife. I don't believe for a minute she left Kent of her own accord. I *will* find out who took her, and God will have to help the person. I won't."

She stepped back, her hands in a defensive posture, and allowed him to swing his leg over Storm's back, but her pout had never been more evident. "I *will* miss you, Jonathan. If only…"

"I didn't anticipate hurting you in all of this. Never. But Payton is the only one I love. The only one I ever will love."

No longer smiling, her expression hardened. "Of course, Jonathan."

Payton wiped webs from her face and held tight to Winter. In a few hours…home. Home! She could picture Jonathan waiting for her with open arms, arms she could curl into and be lost for days. She had already been lost. How many days? She shook her head to clear the muddle that had undermined her thoughts for the longest time. Did Anne tell her Jonathan had been happy she left him? Is that what she'd said? Oh, why couldn't she remember anything with any clarity? It all seemed like one very long nightmare. Nothing but imagined conversations, dreams and fantasies.

An owl swooped down close to Winter, and the horse balked. Payton clutched her mane, but the lack of coordination and inability to keep her feet secure sent her spiraling over the top of Winter's neck. She landed facefirst on a rotten log, barely off the side of the road. Pain shot through her chest and stifled any attempts at sucking air back. A cursory clutch of her ribs offered more searing pain. She fought to speak, cry for help, but words proved impossible. Winter walked back, dipped her neck and snuffed at Payton, but as soon as the owl hooted, she jerked her head up and sprinted away. Soon, there was nothing for Payton but the black of night.

Jonathan's unexpected visit to Wallace Fitzhugh in London produced little more than an uncomfortable situation. He could have sworn Fitzhugh wasn't even aware Payton was missing. Having exhausted all avenues to find Payton, he started for home, the one place that offered a modicum of peace. God seemed so far away from him. Didn't He want Jonathan to know happiness?

He strained to see in the dark, grateful the horse instinctively knew where they were headed. Jonathan lessened the pull on the reins to afford Storm his first break all day. After all, Jonathan had nothing to hurry back to. An empty house full of servants and a succession of lonely days and even lonelier nights. Perhaps he should have stayed in London or stayed with Anne and her mother. He would have at least been around friends and family, but no. Nothing and no one mattered to him but his darling Payton. And Anne's behavior had grown more and more peculiar.

Storm pranced and Jonathan tugged on the reins to control him with the bit; the animal stopped and pawed at the ground. His head swayed from side to side as he kicked up dust.

"What's the matter, boy? It's all right. Let us be on our way." Jonathan patted the horse's neck but to no avail. Storm reared, all but sending Jonathan off his back.

Jonathan slid from the saddle and held the reins tight in his hand. "You see something? There's nothing to be afraid of." He listened for any noise that might have frightened his horse. He rubbed around the wiry hairs on Storm's muzzle and spoke soothing words, doing his best to calm the beast. "There's a good…" He stood still and listened. "Wait. You hear that?"

Storm stomped the ground again, his eyes rolling, the whites showing boldly in the darkness.

Jonathan whirled to the sound of choking. He pulled the pistol from his greatcoat and stood his ground, knees bent, legs ready to spring at a moment's notice. "Show yourself."

Crying. More gasping and strangling noises.

He looped the reins onto a branch and stepped off the beaten path. In two strides, his boot tripped over a log and he bent to move it aside. A hand touched his leg. He jumped back.

"Help me...please."

His eyes narrowed as he stared into the darkness. He tried to focus. A boy? "Here now." He grabbed the hand and turned him over. Eyes, swollen and questioning, stared at him. Air catching in his throat escaped in a loud gasp. "Payton?"

Only one word—"Jonathan?"—sighed through her lips before he dropped onto his knees, cradling her in his arms. He brushed the hair from her face and clutched her so protectively he thought he might be causing her more harm than good.

"I...can't breathe...very...well."

He immediately lifted her in his arms and strode to Storm. "Can you put your leg over?"

"I'll...try." She hoisted her leg over Storm's back, then she wheezed, shuddered and fainted. Jonathan maneuvered her so she leaned over Storm's neck, and he swung into the saddle behind her. He kept his hold to a minimum so as not to injure her further but drew her into his arms, resting her head against his shoulder. He sucked back a deep breath, exhaling through tight lips, and nudged the horse for home.

# Chapter 15

The dream again. Payton wanted to scream because it seemed so real. As if Jonathan was embracing her in a safe, sheltered cocoon, but she knew better. She'd been having the dream for days, weeks, maybe even months or years. Always, Jonathan held her close, his chin nuzzled into her hair where the warm breath fluttered over her. It couldn't be. He hated her. Anne told her how much he hated women. He had killed his own Alithea because he was so jealous of her friends. He was glad when Payton's uncle took her away; Anne said so.

The rocking calmed her body, but her head continued its fitful wandering. "Anne?"

"Anne? It's Jonathan, dearest. I'm right here." A hand soothed her forehead. A hard yet gentle hand. She tried to see whose it was. It couldn't be Jonathan. Could it?

Over the past few days she had awakened dozens of times only to be disappointed when Jonathan was nowhere near. Not willing to succumb to the frustration, she squeezed her eyes shut, forcing the illusion away. Jonathan didn't want her back. When she was ill at... Where had she been? Edgar kidnapped her and then she went with someone. Where and with whom? Anne? Oh, why couldn't she remember what happened to her? Her head ached. The hand again and then the rocking, which sent her into longed-for sleep.

Payton recognized the hands plucking at her. She had felt them before, after the fire. Fingers sent pain shooting through her body. "No," she cried, but the touching continued to torture her. "Hurts...so badly."

The pain grew more intense. Hands turned her and throbbing filled her chest and throat. She leaned over the edge of the bed and vomited. Mallets hammered into her head, the pounding so real she couldn't move. People screaming her name. Her head ached. Light caused more throbbing behind her forehead, and she pinched her eyes shut even tighter so that her breathing constricted along with the muscles. She had died and gone where no one wanted to go. Fire burned her hands and feet and she searched for her puppies in between the flames. *Where are they? Did they all burn? Why am I here, God? I love You. I know I shouldn't be here.*

The voices softened. One in particular was familiar. "Miss, are you all right?"

*Of course not, but no one's listening to me.* "I'm cold. A quilt?"

"You may have all the quilts you like, miss. Do you know me, dearie?"

She had heard the soothing voice. No, her mother was dead. "Mrs. Brewster?"

"You're home, child. Jonathan's outside the door. He hasn't budged from your side for a week."

"I've been...home a week? Why don't I remember?" She sucked in air, but it burned her lungs and her side. "Mrs. Brewster...my head aches and my chest hurts... when I breathe."

The old hands cradled her head and caressed the taut muscles at her temple. "You have three broken ribs and a bump the size of a goose egg on your head."

"My ribs?"

"Yes, dear. And more bruises and scrapes than a rowdy farmhand."

Payton tried to rise up on her elbow, but the pain ricocheted through her chest and drew her back. Before she could gain control over her body, she retched again into the metal pot next to her bed. "My head...swirling and flashing bright."

"There now. Here's a cool rag. I'll go fetch the master."

The cold, wet cloth felt good against her tormented skin, but it did not affect her tormented heart. She was afraid to see Jonathan. Would he be glad she'd come home?

As she waited, a small whimper at her side reminded her again where she was. "Come up, you. I...won't tell... anyone."

And with that, Hope leaped onto the bed and buried her nose against Payton's side.

Weak, Payton lay against the pillows, her color nearly as white as the pillowcase. Jonathan could not stop the fists forming at his sides when he strode to her bedside. The smell in the room revealed that she'd been sick so many times he'd lost count. And it was too stuffy for anyone to heal properly in spite of what the doctor had told

Emily. He walked to the window, drew the drapes back letting in glorious sunlight and opened it to air the room.

Emily grabbed his arm. "Sir, Dr. Finley said you must keep the drapes closed."

"I don't care what Finley said. She needs light, needs to see the world again." He turned and directed his steps to Payton's bed. He knelt by her side and murmured close to her ear, "Is that better, my darling, my beautiful Payton?"

She licked dry, cracked lips and whispered, "Better."

He slipped his arm under her head and offered cold water to ease her parched mouth. "Darling, do you know where you are?" His face contorted and his throat choked shut. If she remembered, she might want to leave him again. Never! He wouldn't allow her two steps from his side.

She fell back against the pillows with a sigh. "Home?"

"That's right. May I ask you something?"

"Of course…anything." Her breathing still labored and her words grew faint whenever she tried to talk, but he had to know. Who was lying to him?

He squeezed his eyes, trying to form the right words. He could kill a man with his bare hands, but here with Payton, he didn't have the vaguest idea what to do. He only wanted to hold her, caress her, kiss away her fears. Each breath she took came at a high price, and he recognized how fragile her condition was. He listened to her struggle as he sat next to her.

His heart tightened in his chest; his hands grew clammy and cold. If only he could hit something, he would feel better. He imagined Wallace Fitzhugh's face. Had Fitzhugh lied to him when Jonathan was in his home? Surely there was a person out there who had the answers.

Payton's eyelashes fluttered against her cheeks, eye opening and closing, and he understood her pain. He couldn't endure the strained expression any longer. His hands danced over her forehead, and he rubbed his thumb gently over her brow and down her cheek to calm the knotted muscles.

"What...did you want to ask me?"

"Never mind. Now that you're going to be better, we'll talk later." She offered a grateful smile as her lids finally drooped.

He tucked the covers beneath her chin, shook the rag until it was cool again and placed it on her head. His eyes suddenly heavy, as well, he headed to the chair in the corner, where he stretched his long legs out on the rug. Hunter sniffed at the leathery boots; he draped his muzzle and paws over Jonathan's ankles, where he closed his eyes and tendered a friendly growl along with a whoosh of warm breath. There was no hurry. Payton had returned home where she belonged. She could sleep all she wanted to. There would be plenty of time to ask the challenging questions.

Payton opened eyes filled with sleep, but what she recognized as refreshing slumber, not the sleep of the dead she'd been experiencing of late. In a minute her gaze adjusted to where she was. Jonathan's home. She sighed. Her home. Their home. Her stomach rumbled, and she sat up, reaching for the dressing gown draped over the chair. She ran her fingers through her hair, now starting to grow out at the sides, and struggled to stand. She faced the mirror. So thin she hardly recognized her own image. The cheeks lacked the rosy-pink of summer. Her body had lost the shapely silhouette she had just begun to develop, and her eyes lacked the luster that had caused her father to say they were the brilliant blue of flowers. *Oh Father, I miss my family every single day. They were my life. And now Jonathan is my life. I pray he still wants me.*

A smile tilted her lips. Her fingers traced the delicate lines of the silver brush she lifted from her vanity. What if he was still simply protecting her? Just brought her back to take care of her? After all, he had made it clear except for the one moment by the brook, perhaps a lapse in judgment, that he was only trying to keep her from her uncle. Wasn't that what Anne had alluded to? That Jonathan didn't really love her?

She threw the brush across the room, narrowly missing a porcelain vase.

Her head ached again, and she slumped into the chair, wringing her hands. Why couldn't she think clearly? She remembered only bits and pieces of the past few weeks. Anne telling her Jonathan was happier without her. That he had moved on with his life. Then telling her he was dead. Oh, why was everything so muddled in her mind?

She loved Jonathan more than anyone or anything, and all she wanted was to live at Kent with him for the rest of her life. To have babies, be a family. Give him the loving home he had wanted with Alithea. She ached for him to love her back with all his heart.

Well, she knew one thing—she was tired of everyone telling her what to do. Her mind would clear and then she could decide what *she* wanted. Whether or not she stayed at Kent would depend on Jonathan's love, not his pity for a helpless woman who had nowhere else to go.

Jonathan rode Storm until his leg ached. He'd spent the morning visiting tenants, doing his best to meet their needs. Having ignored his people far too long, he understood he had to make it up to each one. He would spend the next few weeks while Payton was on the mend tending to his properties. He owed his tenants that much... and more.

With Whittard dead, Jonathan believed Payton to be safe at last. But he still didn't understand where she had been all this time. Relying on his tenacious nature, discovery would come. And he had to know before anyone had a chance to hurt her again.

Flowers had begun to sprout from the ground and leaves from the trees. The fields, being turned for planting, cast green speckles every which way, and Jonathan longed to jump off Storm and sift dirt through his fingers. As he drew from the strength of the land, each of Storm's strides brought him closer to an idea.

An assembly. A party to let his friends know he was ready to move on. All of his friends would be expected to attend. And before the night of the gathering ended, his grasp on who had helped Whittard to bring harm to his wife would be more clear.

# Chapter 16

Payton rested her head against the wall, waiting...for what? This morning Jonathan had begged her to remain in her room until evening. Unsure what he had planned and still feeling tired, she decided to do as she'd been told. For once.

He had assured her they had a lovely evening planned with friends. Whose friends? Most of Jonathan's friends were barely acquaintances of hers. Well, there were Mr. and Mrs. Hathaway, friends of her mother and father. Delightful folks who cared for her, of that she was sure. But why all the mystery? He had been adamant about her keeping to herself while on the mend and nothing strenuous, which ruled out her rides.

Without another thought to what Jonathan had arranged, Payton slipped beneath the hot water and squeezed lavender-scented soap through her hair. The sides had grown in nicely, and now she could pull her hair up with curls dangling over her ears.

The beautiful gown Jonathan had brought from Colchester lay across the bed waiting for her to step into its billowy softness. The deep emerald against her almost-black hair contrasted nicely, and she knew she would appear at her best. Would Jonathan think her beautiful?

She was afraid of him as a child, intrigued by him after her home burned and now very much in love with Jonathan Lambrick. How life changed in an instant. Hers more than most, and she was the most blessed girl in all of England if Jonathan chose to keep her as his wife.

Payton rubbed her arms with the mild soap and languished in the luxury. Would her parents have been happy she had married the master? Of course they would have. Their marriage had convinced her that marrying only for love brought happiness. But did Jonathan feel the same about her?

She dipped under water once again and rinsed the soap from the long curls swirling about her shoulders. Her fingers wiped water from her eyes. The memory clouded her vision more than the soap. Swimming through the water after diving from the sloop. She'd nearly lost her life that night, but escaping from her uncle had been more than necessary—it had been a must. If she had stayed with the two of them... She shivered in spite of the hot water caressing her skin.

The way he had looked at her. She doubted that he was her uncle. No man with any worth looked at his niece thusly. Father had been such a good man, nothing like Edgar Whittard, if that was, in fact, his true name.

Jonathan paced the great hall with sharp steps that echoed. He flinched at the noise. Emily had chastised him as a child for his heavy foot. "Not proper to cause noise like a hooligan, young man."

Hooligan? Edgar Whittard had been a hooligan, for certain. Whoever did that man in had done the world a favor. He shook his head. No...the man was still a human being. He hadn't deserved to be killed. No one deserved to be murdered in his own home.

Behind him, the Comtoise clock struck two. By three, the hall should be filled, and by four, he intended to have answers.

Before his guests began to arrive, he prepared himself with prayer and patience to greet them with the broadest smiles. One by one he planned to pull each aside and dig his way to the heart of what had happened to Payton. Ideas whirled in his head, but he needed to know the truth. No accusations without proof. That was how Emily had instructed him in his youth. And with that thought filling his head, the first guest arrived.

Anne and an assembly of five others. Two women and three men. Evidently, she had come prepared to face off with Jonathan because Dowdy and Fitzhugh were part of her party.

Once they had tidied themselves, he extended a hand. "Welcome, Anne, dearest. Wallace, Patrick and Breighan McCarty, isn't it? And who are these lovely creatures with you?" He fingered the scar on his face as he stared into Patrick's gaze. If only... Not yet. He had to be sure.

Anne broke into a coy grin as she introduced two not-so-lovely creatures to him. Was she trying to appear even more beautiful with plain women at her side? "Jonathan, I'd like you to make the acquaintance of Miss Rosalie Duckworth and her sister, Miss Marianne."

He bowed and scraped. Murmured pleasant greetings, all the while keeping his gaze leveled at Anne. What plans whirled through her head like flapping geese after a choice morsel? Well, Payton was not someone's morsel.

Anne stepped close and put her hand on his arm pos- sessively. "Darling Jonathan, how have you been? I've been faint with fatigue for all of the heartache you've been through these five years. First my dearest sister, and now this. How are you holding up against Payton's disappearance? I do believe should she be all right, she would have found her way home by now."

Jonathan cocked his brow. "Found her way home?"

Anne's fingers dug into his coat. "You know what I mean, darling. Payton would have returned home had she wanted to be discovered. I fear she's fooled you with pre- tense. Her affections were less than honorable, and now she has escaped the nest for her next conquest. Perhaps a man of more wealth, more position."

Her words, like venom, slithered under his skin, and in that moment he understood with certainty that Anne had played a part in Payton's disappearance. He glanced up into Fitzhugh's face, then Dowdy's. McCarty's foot tapped an impatient rhythm as if he longed to move be- yond such talk. Which of them had helped Anne? Or perhaps it had been one of the ladies attending her. His hands tightened. He'd handle this. One minute by one minute, allowing each of them to dig themselves deeper into their pretense. Before this night was over, he in- tended to expose the guilty party.

"If you please, Emily has placed refreshments in the other room. Duncan will help with your things while you refresh yourselves." He patted Anne's hand, felt the cool assurance of a woman with a lying tongue. "What say you, Patrick? You have enjoyed many a meal here."

"Aye, my friend. I have that."

Jonathan lingered over Dowdy's words. He had been here when Alithea died. Jonathan, suspicious of Dowdy, had chased after them to bring his wife back. The man had nerve to show his face at Kent.

Anne's smile shone brighter than the stars. "Oh, Jonathan, I do believe you are ready to move forward. How I have longed for this day." She dropped a gaze in the other ladies' direction. "Come along. Emily always prepares all my favorite foods." When she winked at Jonathan, she added, "I have no doubt there will be blackberries. With dainty little butter cakes and tarts. Am I right?"

"No doubt," Jonathan answered. "No doubt whatsoever, Miss Anne."

Payton waited patiently. She was to remain in her chamber until Clarisse came for her. But why? She should be welcoming their guests alongside Jonathan.

Another glance in the mirror assured her that her husband would shine with pride.

Sitting on the edge of the settee, she rolled the past few weeks over and over in her head. Would Anne be present? She longed to thank her for caring for her at Newbury. Payton might have died at Whittard's hands if not for Anne taking her in. But the memories clouded. Her dreams had created a world of disbelief. Hadn't Anne helped her with Winter?

No…yes! She had. She had put Winter's saddle on, right? But why? Surely Anne could have seen Payton was in no condition to ride.

Payton's head ached trying to remember all that had transpired once she'd jumped from the sloop, but huge gaps filled her recollections and tore her from truth to truth. Perhaps, if Anne came today, she would fill in the big, empty spaces. Before her thoughts could tear her in two again, Clarisse knocked on the door.

* * *

Jonathan awaited his wife at the foot of the stairs, but his gaze wasn't on the beautiful woman ascending the steps. No, his eyes watched the faces of those standing next to him.

Anne's jaw dropped as did Patrick's. "But she's dead," Anne blurted.

Jonathan grasped Anne's arm and twirled her to face him. "And how would you know that, Anne?"

"Well, she's been… I mean…she's been missing. Gone. And now she's returned here?"

"You know full well she tried to return here. You saddled her horse for her. You even purchased Winter from the man Edgar sold her to. Now what makes you think she didn't come home, Anne, dear?"

"But…I saw her."

Patrick pulled her from Jonathan's hold. "Shut your mouth! Do not say another word, Anne."

Toward the bottom of the staircase, Payton stopped. "Jonathan?" And then she started to fall.

He leaped the three stairs and caught her. "Payton, darling?"

Her lids fluttered, all the while Patrick and Anne shouted from one to the other.

"You fool! You said she wouldn't make it back alive," Anne screamed at him.

Patrick yanked her arm until her face lost all color. "You didn't give her enough. Never leave to a woman a man's job."

Jonathan cradled Payton in his arms, but it didn't stop him from confronting Patrick Dowdy. "Enough of what, Patrick? What did you give my wife?"

Anne lost her footing, sliding onto the floor. "She was so sick. So full of laudanum. She shouldn't have arrived home." Her face, the color of snow, couldn't hide what she had done. As her gaze sought Dowdy's face, Wallace stepped away, putting space between himself and the two foolhardy plotters.

"I swear, Jonathan," Wallace stammered. "I knew nothing of their plans and actions. The only thing I *ever* did was to kiss Alithea." As soon as the words left his mouth, he stopped, stared and backed farther from them. "I mean. She kissed me. Uh, I…"

Jonathan called for Mrs. Brewster to take Payton into the great room. He stood to his feet. "Wallace, you have one chance to tell me about your relationship with Alithea. If you don't, I'll shoot you where you stand."

Apparently Wallace believed him. "You see—"

Anne scrambled to stand and clawed at Wallace's face. "You can't! Not now. I'm so close. You can't tell Jonathan."

Duncan pushed through the crowd and restrained Anne.

Wallace turned to Jonathan. "It started out to be a prank, Jonathan. Just to make you a wee bit jealous, Anne said. I was to kiss Alithea when you came into the room, but then, she and Patrick cooked up a plan. Patrick wanted Alithea and Anne wanted you. Patrick cornered Alithea, and after what happened with me, they thought you'd believe she was…well…dallying with your feelings. Patrick intended to force her away but then you caught up with them. *Not* part of their plan." He glared from Dowdy to Anne. "I swear I didn't know about all this trouble with Payton. I'm sorry, Jonathan."

Anne fought against Duncan's iron hold, but he held tightly. "You!" she screamed at Dowdy. "You killed them for naught."

"Killed who?" Jonathan reached for her, but she pulled back. "Who, Anne?"

"That weasel, Edgar Whittard. Niece or not, he had every intention of killing her for the money if need be. He tried to get money from me when he couldn't get it from you. Patrick had no choice. That's when Payton found me in Colchester."

Jonathan's hands fisted at his sides. "So he was her uncle after all. How can I believe you, Anne? You've done nothing but lie to me." A groan slipped from his lips.

Anne pulled from Duncan's grasp and flew to Jonathan's side. "Don't you see? I did it all for you, darling. All for you." With the last words, her eyes glazed and her mouth flopped open. "You would have restored Newbury, but Alithea didn't care a whit about it. She only wanted you!"

He wrenched her hands from his arms, pressing them tightly against her sides. "And you are the one who tried to frighten Payton away from Kent with talk of Alithea not wanting her here." His hands tightened. "How could you, Anne? After all our families have been through. How could you!"

Anne's face hardened. How had he ever believed her to be beautiful? All the while she was plotting against his late wife, her own sister. He'd been so wrong about Alithea. It was all he could do not to throttle Anne.

"Sir, I'll send Birdie for the sheriff."

"I think that's best. I don't trust what I might do if she stays another minute."

Wallace stepped in. "I'll keep my eye on Patrick. It's the least I can do, Jonathan. I'm so very sorry."

All the while Payton stared, wide-eyed at the interaction between the guests and her husband. Anne had drugged her? No wonder she couldn't remember anything after Anne took her to Newbury. And Mr. Dowdy! "Oh, Jonathan. I'm so sorry about Alithea."

He pressed her into his shoulder. "And it might have been you, as well, my darling."

"But Anne said you only married me because of Father."

"Your father? What about your father?" His frown, like boiling anger, washed over her, frightening her.

"She said that he…he made you promise. Promise to take care of me. If anything happened."

Jonathan cuddled her closer. "When I first arrived at Kent Park, he asked me to be your guardian, as well as your brother's, I might add. It was a formality, Payton. I didn't marry you out of obligation. Don't you see how much I care?"

She gratefully tucked herself beneath his arm. "I'd like to go up to our room, Jonathan. I've had quite enough excitement for one night."

He didn't walk with her; he carried her up the entire staircase. "I'll not let you out of my sight, Payton. Not ever again."

His kisses rained down on her head and, finally, her lips. He carried her gently to the room and placed her on the settee. Then he sat on the edge, gazing into her eyes.

"Jonathan, how could she?"

"Mrs. Lambrick?" He smiled.

"Yes?"

"I don't care about Anne or Patrick or anyone else right now. I only care about you." He lowered his head to hers as her heart galloped a steady rhythm. When she closed her eyes, his lips covered hers, gently at first, then in a commanding manner that told her Anne and Dowdy had better be careful.

# Chapter 17

Winter's sides heaved as Payton pressed her to beat Jonathan and Storm to the wooded glen. She was so glad Winter had found her way home. She turned and laughed as Jonathan and Storm drew closer. The horses' hooves beat into the ground in a thunderous explosion of dirt and grass. At last, they arrived at their favorite hideaway. Jonathan was laughing and reaching for Payton to help her down. Hope ran about them in circles, barking and nuzzling their legs.

Payton bent at the waist, drawing the hound into her arms.

Jonathan patted Hope's head. "You funny little thing." He ran his hand over Payton's shoulder. "And here is my beautiful bride."

"Bride?" She fluttered her eyelashes and grinned. "That was some time ago, Mr. Lambrick."

"*Bride* I said, and bride I mean. Come here." He curled

her into his grasp and led her to a small opening in the trees. Spring wildflowers covered the ground. Mostly violets, but smaller white blossoms dotted in between the violets and greens. Jonathan pulled a length of white fabric from a leather bag and draped it over her hair. He took the hound from her arms and set her on the ground. Then he bent low and plucked a handful of blossoms. He tucked them into the gauzy fabric that trailed over her leather jacket and breeches.

Payton breathed in the delicious scents and smiled. "Well, husband, do I look pretty enough to be your bride?"

He ran his thumb across her jaw before dropping a kiss on her forehead. Her eyes widened.

"Listen. I have a surprise for you."

"A surprise?"

"Over here." He placed a blanket onto the spread of flowers. Tucking her hand into his, he dropped to his knees, pulling her down next to him. "Miss Payton Whittard, when I took my vows days before Christmas, I meant every word. I would be faithful and love you but in my heart was an empty space. I didn't know how to fill it."

She waited for him to continue.

"Then, little by little, you filled that space. By caring, encouraging me, loving me more than I deserved. And now, I want to take our vows again. This time knowing just how much you mean to me."

"Oh, Jonathan."

"Payton, I will love you the rest of my life through all the good but, more importantly, through the bad, as well." He grinned. "I think, perhaps, we've had all the bad, haven't we?" Jonathan dropped a peck on her cheek. "I long to have a life of babies, grandbabies and rides through the meadow with you in leather breeches and boots. I promise to love you and offer you all that I possess. Payton, will you marry me again, today? Here, in front of God and everyone?"

Tears welled in her eyes. This man had become part of her, her better half. A love that wouldn't end. Payton used the end of her veil to swipe at her eyes. "I will marry you again, Jonathan. And I will love you forever…I vow… here in front of God and everyone."

Her arms rose and encircled his neck, drawing him to her. As their lips met, sweeter than the violets beneath their feet, she managed to murmur one more time, her breath mingling with his, "Forever, Sir Jonathan."

\* \* \* \* \*

# REQUEST YOUR FREE BOOKS!

## 2 FREE INSPIRATIONAL NOVELS
## PLUS 2
## FREE
## MYSTERY GIFTS

*Love Inspired*

---

**YES!** Please send me 2 FREE Love Inspired® novels and my 2 FREE mystery gifts (gifts are worth about $10). After receiving them, if I don't wish to receive any more books, I can return the shipping statement marked "cancel." If I don't cancel, I will receive 6 brand-new novels every month and be billed just $4.74 per book in the U.S. or $5.24 per book in Canada. That's a savings of at least 21% off the cover price. It's quite a bargain! Shipping and handling is just 50¢ per book in the U.S. and 75¢ per book in Canada.* I understand that accepting the 2 free books and gifts places me under no obligation to buy anything. I can always return a shipment and cancel at any time. Even if I never buy another book, the two free books and gifts are mine to keep forever.

105/305 IDN F49N

Name _____
                          (PLEASE PRINT)

Address _____ Apt. #

City _____ State/Prov. _____ Zip/Postal Code

Signature (if under 18, a parent or guardian must sign)

Mail to the **Harlequin® Reader Service:**
**IN U.S.A.:** P.O. Box 1867, Buffalo, NY 14240-1867
**IN CANADA:** P.O. Box 609, Fort Erie, Ontario L2A 5X3

**Are you a subscriber to Love Inspired books**
**and want to receive the larger-print edition?**
**Call 1-800-873-8635 or visit www.ReaderService.com.**

* Terms and prices subject to change without notice. Prices do not include applicable taxes. Sales tax applicable in N.Y. Canadian residents will be charged applicable taxes. Offer not valid in Quebec. This offer is limited to one order per household. Not valid for current subscribers to Love Inspired books. All orders subject to credit approval. Credit or debit balances in a customer's account(s) may be offset by any other outstanding balance owed by or to the customer. Please allow 4 to 6 weeks for delivery. Offer available while quantities last.

**Your Privacy**—The Harlequin® Reader Service is committed to protecting your privacy. Our Privacy Policy is available online at www.ReaderService.com or upon request from the Harlequin Reader Service.

We make a portion of our mailing list available to reputable third parties that offer products we believe may interest you. If you prefer that we not exchange your name with third parties, or if you wish to clarify or modify your communication preferences, please visit us at www.ReaderService.com/consumerschoice or write to us at Harlequin Reader Service Preference Service, P.O. Box 9062, Buffalo, NY 14269. Include your complete name and address.

LIDIR13R

# REQUEST YOUR FREE BOOKS!

## 2 FREE INSPIRATIONAL NOVELS
## PLUS 2
## FREE
## MYSTERY GIFTS

*Love Inspired*

# HISTORICAL
### INSPIRATIONAL HISTORICAL ROMANCE

---

**YES!** Please send me 2 FREE Love Inspired® Historical novels and my 2 FREE mystery gifts (gifts are worth about $10). After receiving them, if I don't wish to receive any more books, I can return the shipping statement marked "cancel." If I don't cancel, I will receive 4 brand-new novels every month and be billed just $4.74 per book in the U.S. or $5.24 per book in Canada. That's a savings of at least 21% off the cover price. It's quite a bargain! Shipping and handling is just 50¢ per book in the U.S. and 75¢ per book in Canada.* I understand that accepting the 2 free books and gifts places me under no obligation to buy anything. I can always return a shipment and cancel at any time. Even if I never buy another book, the two free books and gifts are mine to keep forever.

102/302 IDN F5CY

Name _____ (PLEASE PRINT) _____

Address _____ Apt. #

City _____ State/Prov. _____ Zip/Postal Code

Signature (if under 18, a parent or guardian must sign)

### Mail to the Harlequin® Reader Service:
**IN U.S.A.:** P.O. Box 1867, Buffalo, NY 14240-1867
**IN CANADA:** P.O. Box 609, Fort Erie, Ontario L2A 5X3

**Want to try two free books from another series?**
Call 1-800-873-8635 or visit www.ReaderService.com.

\* Terms and prices subject to change without notice. Prices do not include applicable taxes. Sales tax applicable in N.Y. Canadian residents will be charged applicable taxes. Offer not valid in Quebec. This offer is limited to one order per household. Not valid for current subscribers to Love Inspired Historical books. All orders subject to credit approval. Credit or debit balances in a customer's account(s) may be offset by any other outstanding balance owed by or to the customer. Please allow 4 to 6 weeks for delivery. Offer available while quantities last.

**Your Privacy**—The Harlequin® Reader Service is committed to protecting your privacy. Our Privacy Policy is available online at www.ReaderService.com or upon request from the Harlequin Reader Service.

We make a portion of our mailing list available to reputable third parties that offer products we believe may interest you. If you prefer that we not exchange your name with third parties, or if you wish to clarify or modify your communication preferences, please visit us at www.ReaderService.com/consumerschoice or write to us at Harlequin Reader Service Preference Service, P.O. Box 9062, Buffalo, NY 14269. Include your complete name and address.

LIHDIR13R